I0593887

CLOWN WILLIAM

CLOWN WILLIAM

Robin Elno

IE Snaps
by
IngramElliott

Clown William
Copyright © 2017 by Robin Hostetter

All rights reserved. No part of this publication may be reproduced, stored in a retrieval system, or transmitted in any form or by other means electronic, mechanical, photocopying, recording or otherwise, without the prior written permission of the publisher.

Published by IngramElliott, Inc.
www.ingramelliott.com
9815 J Sam Furr Road, Suite 271, Huntersville NC 28078

This is a work of fiction. The names, characters, places, or events used in this book are the product of the author's imagination or used fictitiously. Any resemblance to actual people (alive or deceased), events, or locales is completely coincidental.

Book design by Maureen Cutajar, gopublished.com
Cover design by Jeanine Henning

ISBN Paperback: 978-0-9981659-9-8
ISBN E-book: 978-0-9990573-0-8

Library of Congress Control Number: 2017912670
Subjects: Fiction - Western.

Published in the United States of America
Printed in the United States of America
First Edition: 2017, First International Edition: 2017

A Low Ace
Wichita, Kansas April 1875

"Strap on a gun, plowboy. I'll kill ya for that."

William's heart galloped. The challenger was maybe twenty-five, but his face was chiseled from merciless granite. The stone-faced cowboy had two friends who sat smirking at the situation. One, an older man of around thirty, wore silver trim on his brimmed hat, and the other had a scarred cheek and the misshapen nose of an old unset break.

Except for the idle-handed bartender, William was otherwise alone in the rough-planked saloon.

He had left home three days before, hitching a ride on a supply wagon from his home near the Missouri border. His father had shouted after him, "You're sure to come to a bad end, and good riddance to ya." Now his father's prophecy stood to be fulfilled—but much sooner than William expected.

William had offered to help the wagon driver unload, but the man scoffed when one of William's spasms caused him to stumble against the hitching rail.

"Wait for me in the saloon," the man said. "We leave for Dodge City in a couple o' hours."

William should never have gone into the saloon, but his feet ached and he only wanted to sit for a spell.

Tears welling in his dark green eyes, William held his slim body taut. If he tried to speak, his cursed twitches would make him clownish. His shoulders would hitch and his hands flap. But Granite Face, his gun belt filled with gleaming cartridges, wasn't about to crumble.

"Well, say something, ya clown. Ya was snortin' and winkin' and actin' the fool pretty good a minute ago."

William had to get control of the tension mounting within him, so he slapped the table beside him three times and then tapped his fingers three times on the buttons of his shirt. He now felt steady enough to speak. He had to concentrate to form the words, which made his speech stilted and precise, though the tics that crossed his eyes and made his tongue dart out as he spoke broke up the rhythm of his speech, not in a stutter but in awkward pauses and extra sounds.

"Please, mister. I have a sickness that m-m-makes my body jerk and make funny faces. And sometimes words just pop out of my m-mo-mouth"—his head twisted to the right—"but it is just my tongue playing the same k-k-kind of tricks as the rest of my body." He touched his hand to his chin twice.

"I'd think you'd want to be put out of your misery, hootin' like a damn owl and gaspin' like a fish." The hard face of William's adversary cracked at last into an unpleasant smile as he reached for his gun. The movement was slow and languorous. "Guess I'll do you, and the world, a favor."

The older man wearing the silver-trimmed hat stood and laid a hand on the cowboy's shoulder. "C'mon, Walt. Let it go. He's just a dumbass kid."

"Let go of me, Jesse," Walt said. "This one's mine."

"Why do you want to kill him?" Jesse asked.

"How many men have you killed, Jesse Evans?" Walt asked, not taking his eyes off William.

"A dozen." Jesse scratched his jaw. "White men anyway."

"This kid'll make nine for me," Walt said. "I want me an even dozen too."

"That's the liquor talking. Cool off. We just rode into town and I wanna stay awhile."

"Besides"—the third man laughed, which made a jagged scar roll over his cheekbone like a white snake— "ya can't count the kid any more'n a half."

Walt shook his head. "He swore at me like a man, he counts as a man."

William shifted his gaze between the three men. There might be a way out of this yet. A few windows sawn into the split-log walls let sunlight slant through in finger-shaped beams. William cast an eager appraisal at the openings, but they were too small to jump through. He couldn't run. He was unarmed; he could put his faith in that. Surely the men with Walt wouldn't let him just gun a boy down. William looked at the bartender, seeking confirmation.

The bartender frowned, looked at his own feet.

William's shoulders jerked, hands darting for his hips.

"He hasn't got a gun," Jesse said.

Relief flooded through William. This was his way out.

"Give him yours," Walt said through stony lips.

New terror choked William. "I do not want a g-g-gun," William said. His left shoulder hitched up to touch his cheek. "With my twitches, I am sure I cannot shoot straight."

"Tell you what," Jesse said to Walt. "You give him your gun, belt, and all. Once he's strapped, I'll lend you mine."

Walt smiled grimly and unstrapped his belt— weighed down with cartridges, gun, and holster—and handed it to William. "Put this on, boy."

William shook his head. "I have never shot a handgun

before." He turned his body away, hands clasped behind him. A twisting snake of fear roiled in his stomach.

Walt laughed.

"I think we got us a sissy boy here," Walt said. "Ya shouldn't be hangin' out with the men, sonny. Madame French's is where you belong, for those with pee-coo-liar tastes." Walt leaned his face in closer, nose to nose with William. The gunman's breath stank of rotten meat. "Now strap on that gun or I'll break you in for the whorehouse. Already got my belt off."

William's blood turned to ice. Bullied and beaten since he could walk, nobody had ever done that to him. He was not going to let this road tramp manhandle him. He resigned himself to the idea that he would die, today. He hoped getting shot didn't hurt too much.

Jesse leaned in, positioned the belt on William's waist, and tied the holster down to his thigh.

"Why did you make him give me his g-g-gun?" William's hands flapped away from his sides. "I have no chance in a gunfight. This is murder either way."

"I'm evening the odds the best I can," Jesse whispered.

"I got him to give up his own gun, a stupid move for a gunfighter. My gun is raw to his hand. You're in Kansas, boy. If you're gonna jump and dance like a clown, then you'd better be able to shoot. Might as well find out now."

"Of course I cannot shoot straight. But what matter. God gave me shit for life, so to hell with him and you."

Jesse glanced at Walt and then leaned close to William. "Do you know poker, boy? Bluff your way outta this. Turn your back to him and walk away."

"I know poker. You play the cards you are dealt and you r-r-read the other players." William's tongue darted out and his right nostril flared. "Mister, I have been d-d-dealt low hands my whole life. There is never an ace in the deck for me." His left hand tapped his chin twice.

Jesse stood between William and Walt, blocking Walt's view, and thumbed back the hammer on William's gun. He leaned over to whisper into William's ear. "All you got to do is point and shoot. Just don't touch the trigger until the gun's outta your holster or you'll blow your own foot off." He stepped back.

William's heart hammered as Walt buckled on the gun belt Jesse handed him. The last time he had been this afraid was when a twisting, howling cone of blackness ripped apart his parents' home—board from plank. His father had always thought that William's oddness was willful sin, and trouble with his father worsened after the tornado. Angry and accusatory, certain that God punished the family for William's faults, his father finally forced William to leave home.

"Face me, clown," Walt said. "I got no problem with back shootin' a coward once he's challenged me."

William squared off against his tormentor, and the new weight settled down over his hip. Though he'd never worn a gun before and had no idea how a gun should hang, a part of him, deep inside and far away, liked the feel of it. Strange, foreign, and powerful—like he'd just grown a third hand.

"Hoot," William said, his right cheek pulling tight in a tic that made his upper lip curl.

Jesse stepped away, casting William a squint-eyed smile. Now the storm was within him, raw fear whipping around and tumbling William's thoughts in a thousand directions. God had dealt him an unwinnable hand, and he would spit in the Almighty's eye when he faced him, which he figured would be in about five seconds.

Blood pounded through his temples, howling like a Kansas twister. His sight contracted and the edges of his vision swirled in red, leaving a clear center where Walt stood in perfect focus five feet away.

Walt's hand hovered near the gun in the borrowed, well-oiled holster. The man smiled and winked.

Bastard, William thought.

With horror, William realized he had said it out loud. He knew he was a dead man.

Walt's eyes blazed and he grabbed for his gun.

Conscious thought ripped away like a barn in a tornado, leaving William in a timeless void in the center of the maelstrom. He heard a shot in the distance.

The twister lifted, as all twisters eventually do, and the shock of recoil throbbed through his elbow. His brain felt dizzy and his thoughts muddled. William smelled burnt powder and was surprised to see a curl of smoke twisting up from the barrel of his gun. The ringing in his ears blocked all other sound.

He took a deep breath, and it cleared the fuzzy cobwebs from his thoughts. The air smelled fresh and new like a wisp of breeze after a storm.

Walt lay on the floor, staring wide eyed at the ceiling, his revolver still wearing leather.

"Honk," William said. He slid his gun back into the holster on his second try. His knees went weak and he sat down. "Hoot."

"Damn," Jesse's remaining partner said. "That was fast. Is he dead?"

"Oh yeah," Jesse said, looking in amazement at William. "Well played, son. I never guessed you were anything more'n a shavetailed kid." He undid his loaned gun belt from Walt's limp body and jerked a thumb at the belt William wore. "You keep Walt's rig. You earned it. And I expect now you're going to need it."

"We can't let him get away with this," the third man said, his scar a white jag across the deepening red of his face.

"Yes we can," Jesse said. "That shot'll bring the sheriff. At three against one, and facing down a crippled kid, we don't have a leg to stand on."

"But the kid ain't crippled. My God, he can shoot."

Jesse motioned Broken Nose toward the saloon door. "Never underestimate the power of a well-timed drool." Jesse walked across the saloon but turned back at the batwing door. "Is that stuff about your illness the truth, or were you just suckerin' Walt?"

"The God's truth," William said, raising a palsied hand, palm out.

"Okay," Jesse said. "You told the truth, but not all of it." He and his companion pushed through the doors. "There'll be another time," he said. And then they were gone.

William stared at Walt's body. He wanted to vomit. Just a minute ago that man was alive, he thought. He may not have been much, but now he's nothing. Why couldn't he just have left William alone? He thought of running, but shock rooted him in his chair. It was self-defense; he hoped the bartender backed him up.

He and the bartender stared at each other. The metronomic ticking of the wall clock echoed in the otherwise dead-silent room. The smell of shit rose from Walt's body.

William struggled to make sense of what had happened. He had heard that your life flashed before your eyes as you die. He was never sure he believed it, but maybe there was some awareness of things unseen at the time of death. He wondered how it was that he was still alive. A dread thought crossed his mind: Maybe he was dead. God was always an evil prankster to him; it wouldn't be a bit surprising if God made hell look like a Wichita saloon.

A man wearing a star pushed the batwing doors open. Cherub-faced, yet with a firm step that brooked no argument, he was young for a police officer. A sporty mustache curled into careful points. He wore no coat and had his shirtsleeves rolled to his elbows and went about hatless, with rich wavy brown hair combed back. The butt of his pistol protruded from the holster like a club.

The sheriff took one glance at the sprawled body. "What's going on here, Jim?" he asked the bartender, his voice mellow, conversational.

"Howdy, Wyatt," Jim said, coming around the bar. "It was a fair fight."

William tried to speak, but only grunted, and his face twitched. He looked at the tabletop where a half-empty shot glass glinted.

Wyatt gave William a quick once-over glance and then turned back to Jim. "Did the killer go out the back door?"

"It was him," Jim said, pointing at William. "And faster than I've ever seen. Faster than I've ever heard tell of."

This time Wyatt's appraisal was longer, more studied.

William returned Wyatt's steady gaze with his own, interlocking his fingers in front of him around the shot glass, hands on the table. Stay calm, he told himself. Look peaceable. Then his neck spasmed, twisting his face sideways. Damn, he thought, afraid the sheriff would take it as a challenge.

"Him?" Wyatt asked Jim. "How'd he get involved?"

"Gang of three men. They called the leader Jesse Evans. One of'em got to drinking too much and started picking on this here simpleminded boy."

Wyatt's brow furrowed as he studied William. The sheriff scratched his head. The saloon filled with people as word of the shooting spread.

"I've heard of the Jesse Evans gang. Bunch of no-good outlaw gunslingers, the lot of them. But his men are supposed to be fast."

"That scum there . . ." Jim pointed at the body. "They called him Walt. He wanted to shoot that boy just to put a notch on his gun. Got what was coming to him, I say," he said louder to be heard over the increasing buzz of conversation.

"Both men had their guns holstered at the start?" Wyatt asked.

Jim grinned. "Yep."

"Walt's gun's still in its holster," Wyatt said, eyes narrowed.

William knew they were going to hang him for sure. He doubted anybody back home would be surprised to

14

hear he'd been hanged, but he'd figured he'd get farther than Wichita, though.

His father could fully disown him, and figure that made things right with God.

A portly man wearing a town marshal's badge pushed through the swinging doors. "What's up, Wyatt?" he asked.

Another law man, William thought. How many did they need to arrest him? A man lies dead, and they'll want somebody to answer for it. William felt the noose tighten on his neck.

Wyatt touched a knuckle to the right curl of his mustache. "There's been a shooting, Marshal Meagher." Wyatt pointed at William. "That man shot Walt. Witnesses say it was a fair fight. A clear case of self-defense."

Self-defense. William breathed a sigh of relief. Thank God for a reasonable sheriff. He relaxed and his tongue betrayed him. "Hooty."

William's eye twitched when the marshal shot him a look.

"Did he just wink at me? I don't like it," Meagher said. "Clear him out of here."

"You want him arrested?"

"No, not for a fair fight in self-defense." Meagher waved Wyatt toward William. "Just run him out of town. I'd best bust up this crowd before someone else has a go at the kid. People are packing around like wolves to a dead bear."

Wyatt walked toward William, easy and relaxed. His hands stayed at his belt, thumbs curled over the top of the leather strap, fingers well away from his Remington pistol.

William's shoulder dipped in another spasm, and Wyatt flinched, his hand starting for his gun. William closed his eyes and exhaled with an audible effort. He had to stay calm, not give the sheriff any reason to get hostile. He forced himself to keep his hands away from the unfamiliar weight at his waist. He clutched the shot glass harder.

When Wyatt pulled a chair over from a nearby table, William relaxed and gave room.

"Take it easy, son," Wyatt said. "Let's you and me talk."

"Hard for me," William said. "But go ahead."

Wyatt looked into William's eyes. "You're too young to have seen the war or witnessed much killing. How old are you?"

"Twenty," William said, holding Wyatt's gaze. The eyes were stern, but without judgment or anger. Wyatt's mustache smelled of palm oil.

"What's your name?"

"William."

"Got a last name?" Wyatt rolled his fingers in a hurry-up gesture.

"I did, but my Pa took it back," William said.

"Where're you from?" Wyatt asked. "I got handbills I can check."

"Kansas." William grew uncomfortable at the continued attention, though he did not expect it to stop any time soon.

"Hell, boy. We're all in Kansas." That same rolling of the fingers. "I mean where from in particular."

"Near the Missouri line." It hurt to think about home. "No matter. I am not wanted there—not by family or the law either."

"You ever killed a man before?" Wyatt asked.

"No. Never had to. I am not a gunfighter."

"Well, now you've killed a man. Leave town, go somewhere else."

"Why? I did nothing wrong. I just d-d-defended myself."

"It ain't that," Wyatt said. "You stay here and there'll be more killing. It's my job to keep the peace, and I can't do my job with you around."

"I want peace too. Hoot, hoot."

"See, that's what I'm talking about," Wyatt said. "Doing things like that is just going to draw trouble to you like flies to a horse."

"I cannot help it. God saddled me with this s-s-sickness. Where can I go where I would not find trouble?"

Sighing, Wyatt rubbed a hand over his brow. "How'd you get so fast, anyhow? If you didn't want to be a gunfighter, then why'd you work on your draw so much?"

"I did not work on it," William said. "Never owned a handgun before."

"Then you're either the coolest hand I've ever seen," Wyatt said, "or the biggest liar."

"Snot," William said.

"What?" Wyatt said.

William saw Wyatt slide his hand under the table. Fear that the sheriff might be drawing his gun gave William's thoughts sharp focus. William formed each word with great deliberation. "I . . . am . . . not . . . a . . . liar."

"Then why'd you get into a gunfight with Walt? Weren't you scared?"

"Hell yes I was scared. Jesse strapped the gun on me, and then everything happened so fast I just drew and fired." It was just now sinking in. William realized he'd actually been in, and survived, a gunfight.

"I heard what Jim said. No one can be that fast without practice." Wyatt stared a hard challenge.

William shrugged. Maybe he'd been dealt an ace after all. A low ace. He said nothing, but wondered what dirty tricks God had planned for him now.

Wyatt took a deep breath. "As fast as you are, there's going to be people who want to try you. And others who want to watch. I'm curious myself. Well, not in Wichita."

"I am sorry, Sheriff. If I give you the g-g-gun, would you let me stay in Wichita?"

Wyatt again knuckled his curling mustache as he thought. "Cat's out of the bag now. And the story will only grow in the telling, especially if you stick to that yarn about this being your first gunfight. These fellas forced you to put on a gun, the next ones will too. There are some actions that change your life forever, steps from which you can never return. You're a gunfighter now, like it or not."

"I do not want to be a g-g-gunfighter," William said. Horror shrouded his shoulders. Would this scene be repeated everywhere he went? Maybe he had been just lucky with Walt. Maybe he would die in the next town.

Would they send his body home, or just dump it in a hole scratched out of the earth?

He watched two deputies pick up Walt's body and carry it out. "D-did he have a family?"

"Who? Walt?" Wyatt seemed taken aback by the question. "Not around here." He paused, studying William's face. "This really was your first killing, wasn't it?"

William nodded. He saw sadness, without pity, in Wyatt's face. It was a father's look, one that William had never seen before, but he knew what to call it. Compassion.

The emotion fit into an emptiness in William as smoothly as a bullet in a six-gun's chamber. He was thankful to Wyatt for the feeling and would not risk souring the moment. Better to leave one town, William thought, one place, as his own master.

William stood up. "I am leaving."

"There's a lot of room out west, William. You'll find a place."

"I just want a place where people will leave me alone," William said. "Just want to find peace, if God will grant me that this side of the g-g-grave."

2

The Railroad Wars
Trinidad, Colorado January 1878

William began the last year of his life on an open flatcar that rocked as the Chinese workers crowded around him. His clothes smelled of wood smoke, and his hands were covered with soot. He carried all his worldly possessions in a small leather sack slung over his shoulder or worn on his belt. His breath steamed in the cold air. He stumbled and a "hoot" escaped him.

"You owl spirit man," one of the Orientals said. "Bring good luck."

A younger man, his hair in a short braid, waved his hand in front of William in several rapidly sketched signs. "You evil, filled with demons."

William's hand dropped to caress the butt of his revolver. "Maybe I am."

He grimaced, thinking of the past three years, of the string of towns that seemed peaceable enough. But each visit ended the same way—with challenges to a gun fight, William's smoking gun, and the law's orders to leave.

Now the train rolled by the edges of Trinidad, Colorado, and the noisy, freezing ride was nearly over. With a shriek of tortured brakes, the supply train shuddered to a halt.

A burly man with ginger-colored hair climbed aboard. "I track boss. Grab sackees and follow," he yelled at the milling Chinese. Then he saw William and stared.

"You ain't no coolie," he said. "Whatcha doin' back here? Why dinna ya ride in the front with the white folk?"

William swayed even though the train had completely stopped. "Needed to save on the f-f-fare," William said.

The track boss startled. "You sick or somethin'?"

William sighed at the repetitive first impression. "It is not contagious. You said you are the track boss? I am looking for work."

The large man looked William up and down. "Can't use ya, son. Ya might try the Atchison, Topeka and Santa Fe." He jerked his thumb over his shoulder and away from the nearby rough-cut building on which red-and-gold paint spelled out "Denver and Rio Grande Railroad." A two-story saloon, called the Rio, sat next to it.

"Two railroads in this town?"

"Two laid track in, but only one will go over the Raton Pass yonder." The track boss pointed to the mountain upon whose flanks the town of Trinidad clung. "That's the Sangre de Cristo Mountains, the last barrier to New Mexico, Arizona, and the riches of California."

"Thank you for the s-s-suggestion. Whoooops!"

The track boss shook his head. "I ain't done ya no favor. It's a rough crowd, and a hard job. 'Specially since I sent ya to Griz and the losin' side." He turned back to the

Chinese laborers. "Chop-chop. Get movin'." He stepped down from the flatcar and hurried toward the saloon.

Chinese laborers, bent double under heavy sacks, shuffled toward low-slung wooden shacks at trackside. Several rail coaches disgorged gangs of Irish who swarmed with shouted oaths toward the Rio saloon where the track boss waited. The human tide bristled with braids and red hair.

Heading in the opposite direction, William walked to a saloon, its boards still new from the mill, on the other side of Commercial Street. He saw his reflection in a window; white creases crisscrossed his soot-coated face like a surveyor's map.

The saloon, the Topeka Lil, smelled of sawdust and stale beer. The crowded tables forced a line of men to jostle elbows at the bar. The men wore workmen's overalls and leather; a few carried guns. William shouldered through to stand at the end farthest from the door.

"Whiskey," he said when the barman finally looked his way.

The barman squinted at him and his lips curled slightly. "Are you sure?"

"Hoot damn." William clenched his teeth and waited for the spasm to pass. The barman stared at him. William took a steadying breath. "Why not?"

"That coffin varnish is stuff for the Indians. I wouldn't trust any whiskey west of Kansas City."

"So what are these men drinking?"

"Beer mostly. I got good rum for those with a taste for something stronger."

"I am cold c-c-clear through. Anything to warm me up."

The barman brought him a mug of steaming rum. "This will fix you up."

William took a sip, then another. Warmth cascaded through his gut. It was good. He watched the barman fill a tray with glasses of beer. His first friend in any town was always the barman. This one had not stared too much at the vocal tic, and his advice about the drink was friendly and well-intentioned. Not like many other places he had been. He drank with his left hand, his right hand at his side near his single revolver. The cacophony of laughter and conversation washed over him. He scanned the crowd with his ever-watchful eyes, trying to peg which of the men would be the first to give him trouble.

Job Interview

The barman came back. "Want another?"

"Later. Got anywhere I can clean up?"

"Got a pump out back, but for a hot bath try the P. B. Sherman. It's the biggest hotel down on Main Street."

William wondered if his dwindling funds could handle it. He laid a coin on the bar. "I will go see about it."

The barman looked over William's shoulder. "Leave. Leave now."

"Hold on there." A slurred voice roared behind him.

William turned. A bear of a man, shirt stretched tight over his barrel body, glared at him. "Don't nobody leave until I says so. I want to take this prancing dancer out back and squeeze him a little."

"Griz," the bartender said, hands lifted in a placating gesture. "Take it easy. You're drunk. This is just a sick man. Besides, you ain't used up pretty Charley yet."

"Bah. Got plenty to go around." Griz's greasy beard ran down to intermingle with the curly chest hairs that poked through his shirt.

The bartender called out to the room. "Dave. Where are you? Call your animal off."

His pleas were drowned in the rising tumult as men pushed back their chairs and jockeyed for position to watch.

Griz started forward. He wasn't wearing a gun.

The bartender leaned over to speak into William's ear. "Look, just go with it. It'll be a little rough but he won't kill you. That's what everyone before did, and they're still alive."

William's eyes narrowed as he stared at the approaching bear-man. A fistfight was out of the question. He wished

Griz had a gun. William no longer feared a gunfight, but the aftermath was always the same: move on, you're not welcome here. He blew out a long angry breath. He had such hopes that Trinidad would have a place for him to live and work, but this drunken fool was about to ruin it.

William leaned against the bar to stop his twitching. His hand hovered over the butt of his pistol. "Somebody give Griz a gun."

The room went silent until a sweat-stained tracklayer called out. "A gun? Look, boy, it's just a little rough-housing. No use getting yourself killed over it."

William sent spittle arcing through the air to land three feet away. "Griz, armed or not, if you cross that spit, I will k-k-kill you."

"K-k-kill me?" Griz laughed deep and loud. "You can't even stand up straight."

The bartender stood behind William. "Just gun him down. He's a killer. He never gives *his* victims an even chance."

"I have never shot an unarmed man before, no matter how d-d-despicable."

31

"I'd love to see that bully get what's coming to him. He was a bad one before they sent him to federal prison, and now he's twisted tighter than a wet lariat."

William saw the crazed look of murder in Griz's eyes. "If you have reason to want Griz dead, give him a gun. You will never get a better chance."

"You're that sure of yourself? Okay, but it's my ass on the line now too." The bartender took a revolver from beneath the bar and tossed it to Griz. "Looks like you've finally been called out, big fella."

4

Blood in the Game

William saw Griz sweep the gun from the air. Instantly the black tornado, wherein time stood nearly still all around the center of his focus, descended—and he knew the big man would fire at him the instant he had the gun in his hand.

In the beat of a fly's wing, William's revolver was out of its holster and the hammer knocked back. Without thought, without conscious plan or intent, William's single-action weapon trained on Griz's expansive chest.

Griz's thumb cocked back the hammer of his own weapon as he brought it to bear.

Boom! Acrid gun smoke filled the air and for a moment dominated the stale beer odor permeating the room.

When Griz had grabbed for the tossed revolver, he slightly rotated his body to catch it. Now, his body kept spinning from the impact of William's bullet. Griz crashed to the floor, the revolver tumbling from his hand, unfired.

It all seemed too quick, too unbelievable. The saloon crowd waited, silently, for Griz to rise, for surely a life that large could not have been snuffed out so quickly.

William kept his eyes glued to the crowd. He doubted that Griz had any vengeful friends here, but shock did strange things to men.

Griz's death did not disturb William. He no longer had the urge to vomit when forced to kill. They all had it coming and good riddance.

At last the bartender spoke. "Thank God."

The spell of silence broken, murmurs bubbled up from a score of springs around the room.

William waited anxiously for the sheriff, certain he knew what would come next. Hopes for a job in Trinidad vanished, and he had not even finished his second drink. Well, he might as well get cleaned up first.

William reholstered his revolver and turned to the bartender. "Guess I will go see about that b-b-bath."

The bartender nodded and extended his hand to shake William's. "Be sure to come back. Topeka Lil is the Atchison, Topeka and Santa Fe's saloon in town. People call me Sugar."

Puzzled, William turned to leave. The bartender, Sugar, didn't seem to expect to see a sheriff, even with Griz dead on the floor and all.

Three men stood abreast, blocking his path. The middle one, his hat thrown back and held in place by a cord around his neck, stared at William with flat eyes the color of a gun barrel; a fishhook sneer marred the straight line of his lips. The man staring at William had a revolver with a silvered grip. The others' guns had grips of wood with the well-worn and oiled look that comes from hours of practice. These were railroaders of a different type.

"Well, what have we here?" the man with the silver grip asked. "Why didn't anyone tell me the circus had come to town?"

William let out a long sigh. How many times had he heard that same old joke? And everyone who told it thought himself an original wit.

William's hand settled to rest on the butt of his Colt revolver. "My name is William. Hoot."

"William Hoot!" exclaimed the man on William's right.

The silver-liveried one in the middle brushed his left hand against the arm of his companion. "Let the man speak." His eyes had lost a shade of their flat grey.

"I dunno, Dave," said the one touched. "He sounds like an owl to me. Is that what you are, boy? Some kinda owly bird?"

"Be quiet, I said," Dave barked. He turned to William. "I've heard of a fella, acts like a clown, drifting throughout the Kansas cow towns and Colorado gold fields. Claims he never picks a fight, but his smart mouth riles people, and he kills 'em. That you?"

William nodded, eyes fixed on Dave's.

Dave cuffed the man on his left with the back of his hand. "No disrespect! This man is an artist."

The slapped man cowered. "Jesus, Dave. Just havin' a little fun is all."

"Yeah," Dave said. "That's what Griz used to say. Now we're down a man."

"I am no artist, and I am sorry about your man Griz. The same sickness that makes me look like a c-c-clown gifts me this speed with a gun. I used to be scared when some gunslinger thought to try me. Now, I am just frustrated, for I know that once again I will have to move on. I never wanted to be a k-k-killer."

"Well, you've come to the right place to be one." Dave looked deeply into William's face. "Go get cleaned up. We'll talk later."

5

There Is Actually a Sheriff in Trinidad

Following Sugar's directions, William walked down Commercial Street toward Main. Trinidad was a boomtown, but already a few stone buildings proclaimed an intention of permanence. Scores of feed lots formed a broken mosaic in the fields behind the single row of structures lining the street. Wagon oxen stood in steaming clumps in these rail-fenced rectangles, bellowing as if protesting the arduous pull along the toll road over the Raton Pass.

A boardwalk of fresh-cut timbers lined both sides of

the hard-packed earth street. Small shops, flophouses, and brothels made up most of the trade. Two substantial businesses sat catty-corner from each other, taking up the middle third of the avenue: the large mercantile building of Prowers and Hough and the office of the Barlow and Sanderson Stage Company.

Rounding out the commercial interests, the telegraph office occupied the penultimate spot before the intersection with Main Street. This town had good bones, William thought. And since no sheriff had accosted him yet, maybe a place where he could stay. If he could find work.

The workday was not yet over, but men lounged in the street.

William's tongue got that sudden twitch that told him something was wrong. It could be just another spasm coming on, but if there was trouble of another kind, this was his body's warning. He had heard that for other men, the hair stood up on the back of their necks. For him, this prickliness was his tongue's singular eloquence.

Ahead, Commercial Street dead-ended into Main Street at right angles. The Sherman Hotel sat directly across from the intersection.

A gunshot boomed to his left.

William twisted to drop to his right knee, revolver already out of its holster, scanning the street for the source of the shot.

In the street two men slugged at each other with roundhouse blows while a crowd hooted and hollered encouragement. Some damn fool had pulled his gun and was firing into the air. William holstered his revolver and walked toward the hotel porch.

A man with thin white hair brushed back from a yellowish leathern scalp stepped from the hotel and stood on the porch, looking up the street at the commotion. He wore a gun, an old-fashioned baby-dragoon pistol manufactured before William was born. The light caught a star-shaped flash on the man's chest.

The sheriff was at least fifty, gone fat in the belly. He pursed his lips as he studied the fight, and then turned to give William a glance. He looked away for a moment but turned again to spend considerable time looking at William's gun belt and holstered weapon. The sheriff frowned slightly.

William nodded and eased past the sheriff to enter the hotel. A spasm of his left shoulder threw off his balance, and he almost fell through the open door of the building.

The sheriff's eyes went wide and he sniggered. Then he shrugged and ambled down the street toward the fight, which had become little more than a shoving match.

William, having regained his balance, watched him go.

"May I help you, sir?" asked a voice behind him.

William turned to see a clerk wearing a black-and-white checked vest standing behind the desk commanding the lobby. The man's eyeglasses pinched his nose. Leaning on the desk with his hand near the bell, the functionary looked confused and worried.

William remembered his grime- and soot-smeared reflection in the window of the Topeka Lil. Not the best first impression, especially when entering the biggest and fanciest hotel in town. He looked the part of his nickname. It caught up with him in every town, sooner or later. Here in Trinidad, it would be sooner. The Clown.

"Got any baths?" he asked the clerk, who still looked at him in open astonishment.

William settled for a basin of hot water, which quickly turned black as he washed his face in a washroom off the parlor. He brushed the soot from his hat and set it on his head. He wondered where his next meal would come from. The hotel had a parlor between the stairs and the lobby; he would sit there and think.

The chairs sported cotton prints over wooden frames, heavy with padding that cradled his weight when he sat. The clerk scowled as William moved one into a better position so he could watch the door as he sat. William smelled lavender and linseed oil. There was money in this town, if he was willing to work for the railroad. He had heard they were hiring, but he was not interested in laying rails. Perhaps something tucked away in a back room, bookkeeping maybe. His cheek drew suddenly inward and he said, "Hooty whooop."

Someone giggled.

He took his eyes off the doorway and looked to the top of the stairs. A woman stood there, her hand in front of her mouth. Wearing a hooped skirt and shawl, she looked like a young Queen Victoria, cultured and out of place. He judged her age at thirty, though it was harder to tell with a woman than a horse. The frontier drank the beauty from a woman, turning thirty years into fifty. But this was no frontier woman.

William tipped his hat to her as she descended the stairs. She acknowledged the courtesy with the barest of nods as she left the hotel. William's eyes followed her out. He wondered what she was doing in Trinidad. Maybe she worked for the railroad.

He could recognize a gunfighter on sight; a person wore that profession like clothes. But how would an agent for the railroad dress? Would it be like the Queen of England?

He'd check things out with Sugar and hope the bartender could put him on the right trail.

A Good Offer

A heavy tread on the porch broke William's musings. Dave strode in, cracking his knuckles. He went directly to the clerk and leaned over the counter to speak to him. The clerk nodded and waved in William's direction.

Dave shook the clerk's hand and strode across the hotel's rose-patterned carpet to stand directly in front of William, smiling triumphantly.

William stood slowly. They locked stares.

"Have a word with you?" Dave asked.

William waved slowly toward a nearby chair. "Sit down."

"Thanks. I will." Dave turned partially away from William and sidled to the seat. Dave was relaxed and kept his hands well away from his holster. He dropped easily into the cushions and rested his hands on the padded arms. "My name is Dave Rodabaugh."

William nodded. Dave's face—hawkish, sunken-cheeked, and narrow—fit his thin and angular body. He smelled of gun oil.

"Eeehk shit," William said.

Dave's eyes flared at that and his hand dipped toward his gun. But the gunman locked his fingers into a claw, and his hand trembled.

"Sorry. Sometimes I make noises I cannot help," William said. He waited until he saw Dave unclench. "What do you want?"

Finally, Dave pasted a smile back on his face. "First, I'd like to buy you a drink at Topeka Lil's. We near to had a misunderstanding." Dave's accent was from somewhere back east.

"I have a lot of those," William said. "It is best if I stay off the street most times. They serve drinks here in the parlor."

Dave's eyebrows knitted for a moment. "Come on down and let the gang meet you. Once they do, you'll have no trouble from them. If you want to stay in your hotel after that, all right. But how long can you afford a room here?"

"I will find work." William eased back into his chair. "Every town has a stable."

"You can do better than that. You can go to work for the AT and SF."

"I am no tr-tr-tracklayer."

Dave smirked. "Neither am I, and I work for them."

That sounded promising, for Dave did not have the look of a heavy laborer. This man made a living with his gun, not his muscles. Birds of a feather, inviting him to join the flock? William stood up. "I wanted to have a talk with Sugar anyway."

Dave led the way from the hotel, but William glanced up and down Main before stepping off the porch. The wind had picked up, and it was now too cold for people to be loitering outside. However, there was much movement from one building to another. Light flakes of snow danced in the air, blown in off Fisher Peak around whose shoulder the Raton Pass climbed. Gusts rattled a week-old paper banner, shreds of which still proclaimed welcome to the New Year.

William had hopes for Dave. The gunman seemed to hold William in respect, and his invitation to meet the other men sounded like a promise of camaraderie. William had never had a friend; maybe this was the time. And then there was the possibility of a job.

The interior of Topeka Lil's seemed warmer than William remembered. A fire crackled in the stone hearth that sat across from the bar. The scent of burning pine favorably replaced the stale beer smell. A sawdust-covered bloodstain marked the spot where Griz's body had been.

Dave's two myrmidons were waiting at the bar, watching the door.

William's tongue tingled, and he doubted this was to be a drink among friends.

Dave strode to the bar. He told Sugar to draw four beers. He handed one to William.

"Mike, Dan," Dave said, shoving a beer to each in turn. "You've already met William."

"You said you was bringin' us a new gunman," Mike said. "Is he in, then?"

William twitched. "I am no gunman. Dave invited me for a drink with his f-f-friends is all."

"William, you're not giving yourself enough credit," Dave said with an icy smile that did not reach his eyes. "I know a slick hand with a gun when I see one."

"Why did you bring me here?" William dropped his hand, slowly closing the distance to the handle of his Colt.

"I'm offering you a job. We'll pay you a hundred a month, plus a bounty."

"For doing what?"

"There's one too many railroads in this town. You're going to help us push the Denver and Rio Grande out."

"If I remember all right, I rode to t-t-town on the Denver and Rio Grande," William said.

"Many of us did. But the Atchison, Topeka and Santa Fe has the right-of-way over the Raton Pass. This is the end of the road for the D and RG."

William gazed out into the street. "Then why are they still here?"

"They don't recognize our right-of-way. It will get settled in court someday, but tracks laid will count. Possession is the law, they say." Dave rubbed the side of his nose as he spoke.

"Nine-tenths of the law," William said.

"Good enough odds for me," Dave said.

"So what exactly is my job?"

"We're gonna make sure the D and RG workers leave town. If they lay tracks, we rip them up, or take them over. One hundred dollars clears a lot of tracks."

"What about the law? There's a sheriff in this t-t-town."

Dave's friend Dan laughed, slurring his words. "Sheriff? Won't be no sheriff interested. This be railroad bidness, and the railroad handles problems its own way."

"With you working with us," Dave said, "there won't be a Denver man left by the end of the month."

"I am not a hired killer," William said. "I do not care if the AT and SF *is* the law around here."

"We don't have to kill 'em, just shcare 'em out of town," Dan slurred.

William had a paroxysm of hooting and snorting. His arm knocked over his half-finished glass of beer.

"You're a pretty scary guy," Dave said. "Scary and mysterious."

"Of course, if you do have to shoot someone, there's the bounty. Up to you," Mike said, and sniffed. "You could get yourself a new shirt."

"I do not care how poor I am—I will not kill people for money," William said. "If that is all Trinidad has to offer, I will move on."

Dave looked at him in astonishment. "What kind of job did you think I was talkin' about?"

"Payroll guard. Railroad security. But I do not bully unarmed men."

"How many people you killed, boy?" Dave asked.

"That is a different thing altogether," William said. "Money had nothing to do with it."

"Seems to me that if you don't mind killing a man, you might as well get paid for it."

"I do mind killing a man."

Dave shook his head. "Then why do you do it?"

"Respect. Every man I shot had it c-c-coming." William's face scrunched in a tongue-protruding grimace. "They all died from an acute lack of respect."

Mike palmed his pistol grip. "Dave, let me get rid of this clown."

William turned so that he faced Mike head-on. "A lack of respect, j-j-just like that. A failure to respect my right to live."

"Hold on," Dave said, stepping between the two. "So what you're saying is you want to be feared. Believe me, you'll scare the hell out of that Denver and Rio Grande gang."

"Not feared, not as an end to itself. F-f-feared, so people will leave me alone."

Dave sighed. "There's something else. If you won't

work with us, we can't leave you to work for the other side."

"I work for no side but my own." William stared Dave down. "If that is all you have to offer, time for me to go."

"No need. I thought you wanted to talk to Sugar about something."

"Not anymore. I found out what I wanted to know."

William backed toward the door, eyes locked on the three men.

Dave rubbed his hand along his chin and down his neck as he stared at William. He nodded as he seemed to come to a decision.

"Okay, William. See you around." He turned to the barman. "Sugar, William drinks free here."

"Come back," Sugar called to William as he backed from the saloon. "You're always welcome."

Dan sloshed his words. "You're working for the Eighty an' Essef, remember that." He scowled.

Dave laid a restraining hand on Dan's arm and with a slight shake of his head said, "Not now."

7

Grub

William returned to the hotel saddened by the experience at the Lil. No friends, no job, no prospects. In Trinidad he found one thing that had eluded him before: a sheriff who showed no inclination to order him out of town. If William could just find a job, this might be the place where he settled down at last. Tonight's hotel bill was paid; tomorrow he must find work.

He had nothing against physical labor such as laying track, but most employers thought him unfit for it. He had managed to catch the occasional job mucking out stables, but one look at his sudden tics and no one would trust him with a hammer or maul.

When he had heard the railroad was hiring, he had come to Trinidad looking for something quiet and out of the way. Something clerical, for he was smart and good with figures. If not that, then he would be willing to work as a payroll guard. But never as a hired bully. He hated bullies, had been plagued with them all his life.

He sat in the lobby and stared through the window, watching the street grow dark, matching his mood and memory. Age eight, and held down by four other boys while the biggest pounded on his ribs, laughing, calling him "hooty owl." And his father beating him afterward for crying.

By full dark his rage returned to its glowing ember form, and he tucked it away again. Now he just felt hollow. He was hungry. He sought out the desk clerk. "Where's a fellow eat on the cheap around here?"

"The hotel serves a fine meal," the clerk said.

"I will tell you the truth. I can s-s-stay but this one night. I have no m-m-money."

"No problem, sir. The AT and SF is picking up your bill. Enjoy your dinner."

William's neck spasmed and wrung a "honk" from his throat.

The clerk's eyes went wide and he shied back. "Are you all right, sir?"

William sighed. "I will just get some dinner and g-g-go to bed."

He walked to the dining room where twenty square tables neatly dressed in white linen awaited him. Fellow diners occupied ten of the tables. He selected an unoccupied one in a corner.

The lady he had seen earlier sat two tables away. Like him, she dined alone. She looked at him frequently throughout the meal. Her dress with a blue-and-white flower print gave her a prim and proper look. Maybe she was married to one of the city's businessmen; if so, why was she staying in the hotel? And why was she looking at him?

He cut his steak into small pieces so he wouldn't choke if a spasm came while chewing. His hand palsied and knocked over his water glass. Laughter rippled through the dining room; someone applauded. That's why she was looking. William stared at his plate in bullish concentration. He ate the rest of his meal staring at his plate.

The AT&SF paid for his room and board. He had not asked for this boon, and felt no obligation from it. Maybe Dave thought it would entice him to join his gun crew, or maybe he was just keeping William from working for the other side, but William refused to acknowledge that he was on the AT&SF payroll. Let Dave withdraw the offer at any time; in the meanwhile, William had a day or two to find acceptable work.

The next morning he saw the same desk clerk on duty. "Where is the closest stable?"

"Are you looking to buy a horse?"

"Looking for a job."

The clerk's brows furrowed. "If you want that kind of work, there's plenty to be had, I'm sure. There's the Barlow and Sanderson stage office just down Commercial. They can always use a good hostler. Then there're the stock pens scattered all over out back."

"Thanks. I will try the stage company."

The clerk waved him off. "See you tonight."

William walked toward the stone building that housed the stage-line offices. He heard the whistle of drovers and the crack of whips as oxen were started on their labors. They bellowed in protest at the hard day ahead of them.

A group of five men swaggered down Commercial and veered to intercept him. William counted three guns among them, but they were worn hitched back, like an afterthought.

The armed leader was the track boss from the day before. "Heardja kilt Griz. I misjudged you, shoulda hired you for the D and RG. Well, those tracks are already laid, now that you're taking Dave Rodabaugh's money."

One of the two men not carrying a pistol, his unshaven face covered with red stubble, pointed at William. "Dave's been sayin' you hired on to the Atchison to scare us out o' town. But ain't no way I'm scared of no clown."

"Make the clown do something funny, Sean," encouraged a gun-carrying companion. "Make him hoot."

Sean nodded. He stood six inches taller than William. "Yer gonna dance fer me. And here's the tune." He pumped a drum-shaped right fist into his palm.

"Sorry about this," the track boss said. "But we're gonna convince ya to leave town."

The circle closed in around William.

Six-Chambered Trial

William stumbled backward. His ember of fury threatened to reignite. Same problem, everywhere he went. He could sidestep this trouble, but what would that accomplish? These men did not fear him, and they should.

"Hey look, he won't dance," said one of the gun-toting men encircling William. The man drew a wooden club from behind his back. "So the Santa Fe crew hired him to drive us out. Let's show him what we think of that."

William dodged a roundhouse blow from a fat gunman and slipped under the burly arm that had thrown it, escaping the loose circle. He stepped into the middle of the street and whirled, hand by his gun. He grimaced in disgust. His belligerent stance stopped the toughs for a moment.

William focused on the three wearing guns. The track boss glared at him, and the man with the club shifted to a batter's grip. The fattest of the toughs shuffled back a step to stand directly behind Sean.

"Those of you not wearing guns had best stand c-c-clear," William said.

The two rowdies with guns looked at the track boss with uncertain half smiles. The track boss gave a slight nod.

"Hoot. I do not allow anyone to lay hands on me. This stops r-r-right now."

"You're a clown," Sean said. "You and your jigs belong in a circus. Now you're going to take a beating and get the hell out of town."

The gang rushed William, Sean leading the charge with the club-waving gunman a half step to his left. The track boss's hand started toward his gun.

The tornado blew away everything but the moment.

First priority, the charging gunman closing with swinging club. William drew and fired, slamming the man with the cudgel backward with a hole in his chest.

Thumb back the hammer.

Next priority, the fat gunman who had moved to hide in Sean's shadow. Sean closing with William, to grapple and impair his movements. He shot the charging Sean in the leg. Thumb back the hammer as Sean begins to fall.

While Sean falls, throw a glance at the track boss. Still reaching down for his pistol. Glance behind the falling Sean. Fat gunman coming into view, his pistol out.

Center of mass and fire. The fat man clutches his chest, gun flying from his fist. He crumples.

Thumb back the hammer.

William turned to the track boss, whose fingers were just now touching the butt of his pistol. The man didn't have a chance in hell, and the tornado cleared from William's mind. One moment to decide.

William shot again and grazed the cheek of the track boss, stopping the man's draw before he got into real trouble.

"I am serious," William said. "No one touches me."

"Get him," Sean roared, both hands holding his thigh. "He's broken me leg."

Gun smoking, William raised an eyebrow at the one unwounded man, who held trembling hands up in surrender and backed away.

The track boss tried to help the cursing Sean to his feet, but the huge Irishman was too heavy. Sean was left moaning in the cold street.

Men ran out of the stage office. The street filled with the curious. No one brandished a weapon, but it was just a matter of time.

William had to get out of the open. He needed a place to hole up and see what happened next. William trotted down to Topeka Lil's. For safety's sake, he usually kept the hammer of his pistol on an empty chamber by loading only five cartridges. Now there was just one left in his gun, but he feared to tip his hand by reloading in plain view.

He hoped one was enough to reach cover. Probably few of the onlookers kept count of the shots, and most would assume he had more than one cartridge left and hesitate. They would wait for a larger group—he needed to be under cover by then.

Across the street, men poured out of the Rio and an angry crowd formed.

William exhaled in relief when he got inside Topeka Lil's.

Mike clapped him on the back.

Dave brought him a hot rum. "Looks like a good morning's work."

William refused the drink. "If you had anything to do with that, I will shoot you next."

Cold steel fell across Dave's eyes. Dan and Mike shuffled backward, hands suddenly at their sides, fingers curled above pistol grips. The noisy saloon instantly hushed. In contrast to the sudden silence, a growing clamor could be heard outside.

"Don't ever try it," Dave said. "I never travel alone. It's why Griz worked for me, and not the other way around."

Dan and Mike grunted.

William stared down all three. Moisture beaded Dan and Mike's foreheads.

Shouts outside demanded William show himself.

Dave blinked and relaxed. He inclined his head toward the shouting. "Do you want help with that?"

William slowly drew his gun, broke open the cylinder, and began reloading. "What do you have in mind?"

"The four of us will face them down. It will be guns against fists, unless any of them are foolish enough to try us. I think they'll get the message."

This time William filled all six chambers of his revolver and holstered it. "I will go out first, alone. Better they see they d-d-do not scare me. I will try to talk it out. But I will not let them take me whether you b-b-back my play or not."

Cold and detached, William stepped from the saloon. Boos and catcalls greeted him. He waited stoically, nerved up, joints loose. It had been a long time since he felt afraid when gunplay was imminent. Eventually the crowd grew quiet.

Without a quiver in his voice, William shouted to the

mob. "What do you want with me?"

"You murdered those two men," someone shouted.

William scanned the crowd. The man who shouted was wobbly, his face flushed. Booze and anger. William knew from experience it was a deadly combination. But the man was not one of the five he had faced.

"Were you there?"

"No, but I heard—"

William cut him short. "You heard wrong. Who calls it m-m-murder? Step forward and say it to my f-f-face." An angry susurration passed through the crowd, but no one stepped up.

"Then if there is no accuser, this trial is over," William said.

"Sweeny saw it," someone shouted.

"Which one of you is Sweeny?"

No one stepped forward.

"Then I say again, no accuser, no trial. I will t-t-tell you how it was, and that will stand for the m-m-matter. I was accosted by five men who made to lay h-h-hands on me. They were armed and I d-d-defended myself. No one lays hands on me. I gave them fair warning. Now I give warning to you. Anyone d-d-doubts my word, speak up like I told you before."

No one. The edges of the crowd began to melt away. Dave and Dan strolled out to stand beside William, thumbs hooked behind their belts as they smiled cynically at the crowd. The mob dispersed in little grumbling knots, many retreating into the Rio.

"I think that covers it for the morning," Dave said, returning to the bar with William.

"But not for good, I fear," William said.

Dave shrugged. "Draw two, Sugar."

Setting a beer down in front of William, Dave said, "Maybe you'll have that drink with me now."

William opened the cylinder of his revolver and slid one cartridge out. He snapped the Colt together and positioned the hammer on the empty chamber.

William dropped the retrieved cartridge into the beer in front of him. "No."

Fire

William applied at the stage office that afternoon. He spoke to a fussy little clerk with squint eyes and a large beaked nose.

"Mr. Barlow does all the hiring. Mr. Barlow is not in town at the moment."

"I see. When is he expected back?" William asked.

"Couldn't say." The clerk sniffed.

"Harlot skirts," William said.

The clerk's jaw dropped. "I beg your pardon?"

William stared icily at the clerk. The clock on the wall ticked loudly. The clerk grew red in the face.

"Good day, sir. Mr. Barlow does the hiring. Mr. Barlow is not here today."

William said nothing. He stared even harder at the clerk; then his face twitched and one eye squinted shut.

"You would not be suitable for the job, sir," the clerk said. "We have no need of gunfighters."

William pointed at two portraits of distinguished-looking gentlemen hanging on the wall behind the clerk. "Which one of those is Mr. Barlow?"

The clerk shot a quick glance at the portraits. "The one on the left."

"And the other is Mr. Sanderson?"

"Yes. But he is in Denver. It is Mr. Barlow who does the hiring."

"And Mr. Barlow is in Denver too? And I t-t-tell you it is best not to lie to me."

"No, he is not."

"So what would Mr. Barlow do if something were to h-h-happen to you?"

The clerk's face paled. "Is that a threat, sir?"

"No. I just want to know how Mr. B-B-Barlow can be reached in an emergency."

"Mr. Barlow can be reached by telegraph."

William did not like preying on the fears of others, but he needed to talk to someone in a position to hire him and this fussy clerk was blocking his way. He shelved his qualms and leaned close to the clerk. "Then reach him."

The clerk paled and bit his lower lip.

Satisfied that he had done all he could for the moment, William went back to the hotel. The hotel served drinks in the dining parlor; he ordered hot rum.

The tall and aristocratic barman brought his drink to him. "We also have a fine bourbon if you prefer."

"I was told not to tr-tr-trust whiskey west of Kansas City." William drank the rum.

"I'm talking about bourbon, sir. We bring it from the east through St. Louis by train. I can show you the sealed bottle if you desire." The barman wore a livery of sorts—a black silk jacket and white breeches. He was swarthy, but there was no trace of a Spanish accent.

"Sure, I will try some."

The barman brought him a golden-brown liquid in a cut crystal glass. William sipped the drink. "Smoother than the whiskey I have tr-tr-tried."

The barman snorted. "Of course. This isn't that fire-water that passes for liquor on the frontier. This is good Kentucky bourbon."

"Looks like the railroad brings fine things."

"That it does, sir. It's worth a few growing pains." The barman's face remained grave. William had never seen a butler before, but he imagined they looked like this.

"What is your name?" William asked.

"Samuel Prescott. Pleased to meet you, Mr. Clown."

William choked on a swallow of his drink. "My name is William."

Samuel's face paled. "Oh dear. I am so sorry. The diners have been calling you clown, and I thought that was your name."

"It does not take l-l-long for that name to stick to me in a new town."

"Still, there is no excuse for such a mistake. My

deepest apologies, William. I must speak to Robert, the desk clerk. He should keep me apprised of such things." His stiff upper lip seemed to soften a little.

"It is okay, Samuel. You talked about g-g-growing pains. Which railroad do you favor?"

"No real matter to me. The hotel has been getting its goods through the Denver and Rio Grande, but only for the last few months. Trinidad is on the Santa Fe Trail, after all. The Sherman Hotel has been here since Woolton and McBride built the toll road in 1865."

"They must make a lot of money on that t-t-toll road. What is going to happen to them when one of the r-r-railroads pushes over the Raton Pass?"

"Go out of business, probably. But they've made their money already. I heard they were paid a hundred thousand dollars for the right-of-way by the Atchison, Topeka and Santa Fe."

"So the Atchison really does have legal c-c-claim to the Raton Pass?"

"The toll road part anyway, but I imagine another railroad could blast its own way through using a different route."

"What do you think about both railroads having work g-g-gangs here in town?"

"Good for business, but not if things start getting rough, like the shootings today." Samuel blanched. "Sorry, I forgot to whom I was speaking."

"No harm. What did you hear about the shooting?"

"That a bunch from the Rio Grande tried to work you over, but three of them got killed instead. Clear case of self-defense."

"It was only two got k-k-killed. But the rest is correct. Including the self-defense part."

"Of course, sir," Samuel said.

That night at dinner William noticed a definite change of attitude. People were deferential to him, and if he did make the occasional grunt or grimace, they politely hid their smiles behind their hands.

The young woman, tonight wearing a string of pearls over her black dress, continued to study him, her head tilted to the side, eyebrows furrowing at times. She seemed to be thinking something over. William decided to ask Samuel about her. If she was connected to one of the businesses in town, her interest in him could pay off with a job.

William did not return to the Lil that night—better to leave well enough alone. He went to his room.

He was awakened at three thirty by the clanging of the town's fire alarm. From his window, he saw flames shooting up by the railhead. A fire in the tinder-dry towns of the West threatened everyone, and doing his part in a bucket brigade might distract people from his strange mannerisms. It might lead to a job. He pulled on his clothes and strapped on his gun belt.

10

Losing Control

When William arrived at the conflagration, he saw the Chinese shacks were in flames. The hastily formed bucket brigades ignored them and struggled to put out the burning creosoted ties stacked in neat rectangles. He headed for a place in line but felt someone pull at his elbow.

It was Dave's mushy-mouthed friend, Dan Dement. "You can see better from over here."

"I am not here to look—I am here to help."

"But that's the Dirgee camp. The Eighty and Essef is back this aways." Dan tried to pull him back.

"Let go of me. I t-t-told you no one lays hands on me."

Dan stepped back as if scalded. He stood hesitantly, fingers curling and uncurling. "Let the camp burn. That's why the fire was started."

William's lip curled in disgust. "Where is Dave?"

"Back at the Lil. We got buckets there too if ya want to pitch in. Gotta make sure the Lil don't burn by accident."

Shouts and curses came from the Rio. Some embers had gotten onto the roof of the neighboring station and were starting to smolder. A group of men came out of the Lil and headed toward the rival saloon. "Looks like they are g-g-going to help after all," William said, hurrying after them.

But when he got closer, he could see the group from the Lil were not carrying buckets. Armed with clubs and brickbats, they swarmed onto the straggling line of bucket handlers who were forming up to save the station.

Chaos reigned. William could not tell one side from the other in the smoky light from the leaping flames.

Already, limp forms lay stretched out. Screams, curses, shouts, the roar of the flames—the din was crushing.

Clear that he could do nothing to fight the fire, William retreated to the Lil.

Dave met him there. "Glad to see you could make it. You want a bucket?"

"More of your tricks?" William pointed at the blaze.

"Act of God," Dave said, his eyes twinkling like a devil's in reflected firelight.

"Look, there's some more men over there." Mike pointed at three running figures flitting through the shadows. "Caught with their pants down in the red-light district."

"Head 'em off," Dave ordered. Mike and four others sprinted out the door in pursuit.

Amid the roar of the flames, William heard shouts and clangor and the bellowing of livestock in the pens. Men screamed. The oily stench of burning creosote and more screams, sounding inhuman, filled the air.

The fighting lasted only as long as the rough-planked station. When the roof crashed in with a gout of smoke and a blizzard of sparks, the D&RG men fled.

A cheer went up in the Lil, and Dave passed around bottles of bourbon. "A good night's work." He thumped the soot-stained, bruised, and bloody men on the back as they trudged back into the Lil.

The shouting and coarse laughter made William want to leave. Before he made it to the door, Dan's voice stopped him.

"Hey, look what's comin'." Dan pointed through the window of the Lil.

A band of rough men, clothes singed and blackened, carrying wooden cudgels and shovels, approached. The trail boss led them. "Our railhead's burned," he said. "And you dirty bastards done it. Now you're gonna pay."

Dave stepped from the saloon and into the dim light cast by the bonfire that used to be the Denver and Rio Grande depot. "I don't think so."

Dan moved to stand behind him, thumbs looped casually through his gun belt.

William stood in the doorway, apart from the tableau outside, but noted that the shifting light of flickering flames joined his shadow to theirs in one multiheaded menace.

The angry mob rushed the saloon.

Dan and Dave fired into the crowd.

Some of the mob had brought guns and returned shots wildly.

Since William stood on the boardwalk and out of the street where the melee swirled, he was not directly threatened by any of the combatants. He stood with his revolver in his hand, and watched. His tongue itched and he stepped back into the shadows.

A shotgun boomed.

The dark tornado descended.

William fired. It was as if he watched someone else pull the trigger. The internal maelstrom strengthened beyond levels ever reached before. William's consciousness, his will, ripped into timeless shreds. His gun seemed to fire on its own as targets were selected without thought. Dimly conscious of reaching for another cartridge from his belt, amazement he had already shot six times. Then nothing except a muffled sound like distant thunder.

His first clear thought: he was cold. He stood shivering on the boardwalk of the Lil. Men in the street scattered in a tumbleweed stampede; bodies lay like crumpled rags in the icy dirt.

He didn't know how many men he had just killed, but his revolver and cartridge belt were empty.

Dave stood beside him. "You are one crazy son of a bitch."

William felt naked with an unloaded gun. He helped himself to four cartridges from Dave's belt. He knew Dave was talking to him, but the meaning was not clear.

Dave let him take the bullets. "You were jittering around like a cricket in a hot skillet. I knew you were fast, but gawd almighty I swear you were loadin' and firin' at the same time."

William's thoughts hadn't quite jelled yet. "What happened?"

"What happened? You scared the absolute shit out of everybody."

Pride, like a swallow of hot rum, warmed his heart. He looked again at the bodies in the street. Nausea wiped away the good feeling. Some of the dead had been unarmed.

It had been a mob, he reminded himself. The firing of the shotgun had emphasized his mortal peril. His memory was full of blanks after that. Had he fired indiscriminately into the crowd, or picked his targets? It didn't matter; what was important was unarmed men had been killed. And he did not know if he had done it.

People feared him now, but he didn't feel victorious. "I think I had better get back to the hotel," he said, hands shaking.

He left the saloon and somnambulated down Commercial Street. His head hurt. He felt cold. It seemed a longer walk than usual. There was still a lot of noise and commotion at the railhead, but it was distant to him. Creosote-scented cloud wisps drifted by.

He decided not go to the hotel but wandered into the maze of cattle pens behind the buildings on Commercial Street. The anxious cattle had begun to settle, but were jumpy with the scent of smoke still in the air. William leaned against the wooden railings and watched the stars.

The sky was beginning to pale, and the fainter ones had already faded away.

When Dave had offered him money to kill people for the railroad, he hadn't even given a thought to accepting the deal. But he had allowed Dave to pay his bills at the hotel. That seemed to be making the best of a bad situation; he had never agreed to work for the railroad, and if Dave wanted to throw his money away, well, William needed a warm, dry bed and hot food.

Now he saw it for what it was: a manipulation and a trap. And tonight, he had gone to fight the fire, again with the best of intentions, and been pulled in deeper.

William had wanted to be discriminatory at first, withholding his shots unless directly threatened. However, a shotgun is an indiscriminate weapon; it was as if everyone in the mob was armed. His dark tornado had been unleashed before William even consciously registered the shotgun blast. Yet William had broken his cardinal rule. Unarmed folk were dead.

Growing up under the tutelage of Reverend Hawkins, William had been assured that God had special plans for him. As long as he controlled the evil with which God tested him. God answers prayers, the reverend had assured William. The good man had been a bulwark for William as he tried to find God's purpose in his affliction, and a buffer when his father grew violent.

Watching the slow wheel of stars, William thought back to when he was twelve and the day the minister had given up on him, certain that William was not praying hard enough. The reverend refused to baptize him so long as the tics and verbal outbursts remained unchecked.

Perhaps Hawkins had been right. Perhaps God had made William one of his darker angels, to do his work on earth without hope of seeing heaven. But this business tonight—had even God lost control of his instrument?

11

The Stage Manager

William returned to the hotel a half hour after sunup. He saw Robert at the desk and asked him to go to Prowers and Hough for boxes of ammo. "I will be staying in today. Just put it on the tab."

Robert nodded. "With a slight delivery fee added."

William spent the day in his room. He cleaned his gun, then took it apart and cleaned it again until the barrel was shiny bright. But he still felt tarnished. He felt he had been played like an old fiddle last night, and as he polished his revolver, he knew whose hand was on the strings.

William had the dining room all to himself that evening. Over his meal of smoked fish, he wrestled with the old questions again. Why had God made him different? Had the devil really put his mark upon him? Where was God when that happened?

After supper, William nursed a shot of bourbon in the lobby, watching the sunlight fade, glad for the solitude.

Dave pulled up a chair. "That little fracas last night put the run on most of D and RG," Dave said lightly through a genuine smile. "Soon as the weather breaks the AT and SF will lay tracks over the pass."

William did not acknowledge him; instead, he sat cold eyed and stared out the door, rolling the shot glass between his fingers.

Dave said, "I got some business back in Kansas for the next few days, so Dan, Mike, and me will be leaving things here in town to you. The Rio folks are pretty buffaloed. I don't think they'll give much trouble until we get back."

William ground his teeth but made no answer.

"Well then," Dave said and pushed back his chair.

Now William looked at him, set the shot glass down,

and drew four cartridges from his belt. "I owe you four bullets."

Dave glanced at William's glass of bourbon. "Keep 'em for some other time." He whistled "Oh! Susanna" as he walked from the hotel.

The tall grandfather clock chimed nine times. William saw the clerk from the stage company enter and head for Robert at the desk. Halfway there he made eye contact with William, and veered toward him. The clerk pressed his palms together in a wringing motion. He dropped his eyes slightly when he spoke. "Mr. Barlow is back. He sent me for you."

William stood. "Let us go see him, then."

The clerk led the way down the darkening street in short little steps, constantly looking back over his shoulder at William, and did not relax until they entered the stage office.

There were three other men waiting there. All wore guns, the hammers still tied back. They smelled of sweat and hard labor. Brown mud crusted their boots. One motioned for William to step through the room, pointed to a door to an inner office. "Mr. Barlow is in there."

A man in his fifties sat behind a desk. He wore a suit and western vest. He looked softer than his portrait. "Leave the door open," he said and pointed at the three men in the outer room. "You've met Tom, Bart, and Jasper."

Each one nodded or frowned in turn.

"Some of my best drivers and not afraid to ride a little shotgun now and then." Barlow settled back into his chair. "Now, what can I do for you? What's all this about having business with me? When Copper told me that you wanted to see me . . ."

"Who is Copper?"

Barlow drew a breath. "Copper is my clerk. He telegraphed that you wanted to see me. He made it sound like, well, forgive me, but like his life depended on it. I didn't know what he meant, but then once I got here, everyone was talking about you, and all, and you wanted to see me . . . Well, some say you're crazy."

"He did not tell you I was looking for work?"

"He said it was about a job, and then finding out the kind of work you do, and you looking for me, and well, I thought . . ." He sighed.

"Do you have enemies, Mr. Barlow?"

"Some, but none that would send a hired killer after me."

"Rest easy. I just wanted to ask you for a j-j-job."

"Me? I don't need anyone killed."

"I am not a hired killer, Mr. Barlow. I was looking for a j-j-job with your stage line."

Barlow looked at him with lips pursed and brows drawn. He glanced into the outer office where Tom and the other two hands waited. "Not a hired killer? The D and RG crews are all hanging around by the railhead, afraid to come down Commercial as far as Main."

"Somebody else's battle, not mine. How about that j-j-job?"

Barlow gave him a sour look. "Frankly, I would be afraid to hire you."

Disappointment, its edge sharpened by anger, formed in William's gut. He nodded to Barlow to continue.

"Well, you draw trouble. I can't think of anything that I would ask you to do."

"I can clerk some."

Barlow's face was ashen. "I'd be afraid of you. That puts me in an untenable position as your boss."

"Maybe you could find a place where I w-w-would be no trouble." William's face spasmed.

"Where would such a place be?"

"I am not afraid to ride shotgun either. Or I could run a way station for you. Out in the middle of nowhere, away from tr-tr-trouble."

Barlow looked closely at him. "You don't look like you've got the, uh, muscle to be a hostler."

"Mull it over awhile."

Barlow nodded. His eyes sparkled, and his mouth twitched in a ghost of a grin. "I will."

Jasper escorted William out of the office.

William left and, feeling Tom and Bart relax, thought he would not be hearing from Barlow anytime soon.

Samuel brought William a late-night bourbon. Not a bad life, William thought, sitting here and drinking on someone else's dollar. He wanted people to fear him so he would be left alone; now that was what was happening. But Dave had turned him into a bully and William hated bullies.

"Will there be anything else, sir?" Samuel asked.

Samuel's clipped polite words broke into William's reverie and reminded him of the gentility of his surroundings. And a question he had meant to pose days before.

"There is one thing," William said. "What do you know about the lady?"

"Lady, sir?" Samuel gave him a bemused smile.

"You know the one I mean. She is staying in this hotel. Wears a lot of b-b-black."

"I will inquire if she would like to meet you, sir. That's the best I can do."

William grimaced. He was just curious; he had no illusions about his attractiveness to the opposite sex. "I am not looking for a liaison. I was just wondering who she was and why she is staying at this hotel."

"As you say, sir. But it is not my place to be telling such things. I can introduce you as would be proper in such matters."

"Fine, go ahead and ask."

William drained the last of his bourbon. He held his hand out to judge its steadiness. It seemed all right. But he would have to slow down on the drinking. There was so little else to do.

The next morning he left the hotel to inquire at the stock pens. He liked the idea of managing a stage way station. Maybe he should get more experience with animals, and then try Barlow again.

He had just passed Prowers and Hough when his tongue tingled. He dropped his hand to his single-action Colt and put his thumb on the hammer. A bull of a man stepped from the alley.

"Been waiting far ya." William did not need the Irish brogue to know the man was from the gang at the Rio. He had fierce eyes and a full mane of red hair. He wore sturdy cotton work clothes—and had a pistol belt buckled low on his hip. A handful of his fellows stepped from the alley, and small mercurial droplets of men crossed the street toward them.

"Why wait? You knew where to find me. You should have c-c-come in; we could have had a dr-dr-drink." The droplets of men were rapidly coalescing into a poisonous pool.

"The time far drinking is past. Ya say ya want no one laying hands on ya. Well, I come to do just that. Look, I'm be taking off me gun." The man turned his back, and with slow drama removed his gun belt and laid it in the street. He balled up his fists and squatted into a fighting stance in front of William, corded arms sprung from massive shoulders.

"You're a drunken fool. Go sleep it off." William tried to step around the belligerent bull. The crowd of men laughed.

William stopped sidestepping. "I am warning you and all your friends. I do not f-f-fight with anything except my gun. Best think on that b-be-before you provoke me."

"Ah, 'tis scairt ya are. What will ya do, poor little clown? If ya shoot me, they'll hang ya far murder." He lunged in, swinging.

12

A Handler of Beasts

William took a step back and shot the man in the foot. The man yelled and hopped on his other one. William let the bellowing Irishman see him draw a bead on it. "I would scat if I were you."

The crowd stood in openmouthed silence. Then someone cried out, "Ya shot him, ya dirty coyote. And him not havin' a gun."

William held his Colt steady and thumbed back the hammer. "A fight with me is always a gunfight. You are a fool if you b-b-bring anything less."

Angry murmurs and mumbled oaths percolated around. William eyed them coldly. "Is there no one else? Are you jackals, or men?"

The men hung their heads and slunk off.

William turned down the alley beside the mercantile building and headed into the field behind the city street. He had his pick of stock pens. A third of them were empty. He leaned against the rails of the first one that had livestock. Seven oxen eyed him, their brown eyes distrustful. Cow droppings frozen into flat disks littered the ground.

He had time to sort through his thoughts. Though he had managed to get out of that tight spot, his choices were being ever more constricted, like a trail through a narrow canyon. Here in the West a man lived by his own rules, if he was strong enough to defend them. Every year saw fewer such men, and the law favored the weak. He hoped he had made his point but knew the next showdown must be a clearer case of self-defense.

A broad-shouldered man with large scarred hands and no fat around his middle approached. He wore a scuffed holster, the butt of an old army pistol reaching out like a question mark. His face was dark and sun-lined. He smelled coppery, like new wire. William felt no menace from him.

"Looking to pick out a team?" the man asked, his voice old crows and shoe leather.

"Looking for work."

The man studied William closely. William grimaced and drew a snort from a partially collapsed nostril. The man's sun-mahoganied face paled to the color of live oak. "I know who you are. Sorry. I guess you already picked a team."

William sighed. "You have anything? I can handle animals. And it looks like the p-p-pen could use some mucking out." He waved his hand, his left hand, and indicated the piles of manure.

The man backed away. "Do you take me for a fool? No work. Try over at Sanderson's."

William watched the drover hurry off and then tried several other corrals. No one would hire him. Some seemed just scared. Some favored the Denver, and they were really scared.

William returned to the hotel. He would have to take the AT&SF money, or leave town. Once the fighting was settled, he might parlay his experience with the railroad into a job as a station agent, but he'd have to figure how to get through the next week or so. William took an early seat in the dining room for he wanted only his thoughts for company.

He changed his mind when Samuel brought the lady to his table. She wore a black dress trimmed with yellow ribbons.

"I hope you don't mind if we share a table," she said before Samuel could speak. Her English was the Queen's English. Surprised by her approach, William checked the sight lines to the door and windows. There was nothing unusual, other than the woman asking to sit down. He stood.

Emily

"Please, sit down, ma'am."

Samuel pursed his lips slightly, and his eyebrows drew down as he gave a small shake of his head. William thought he heard a "tsk tsk" on Samuel's indrawn breath.

"May I present Miss Emily Tunstall. Miss Tunstall, this is William. I do not know his last name," Samuel said with a stiff lip and a sniff.

William held his hat before him and inclined his head in Emily's direction. His neck twisted in sudden torsion and wrung words from his throat. "Piss, piss, pissed." He reddened and nearly dropped his hat.

Emily's eyes went wide, and then she erupted in peals of laughter. She sank down in the offered chair, hand at her throat. Little tears squeezed from her eyes. She tried to catch her breath, and the air snorted through her nostrils. She howled in new paroxysms.

William joined her. He laughed as he could not remember laughing before. Through watery eyes he saw Samuel, shoulders quivering, bite his lips but lose his own battle with laughter.

William sank into his chair, and the shared laughter spluttered out in fits and starts. When it passed, all the tension was gone.

Emily dabbed a last tear from between nose and eye with the tip of her finger. "You sure know how to sweet-talk a lady," she said, face scrunched afresh in laughter, making her nearly snort the last word.

"I do my best, ma'am."

Emily beamed at him. "You're a bard's delight."

"Ma'am?" The savory smell of roasted fowl drifted in

from the kitchen.

"A bard: a traveling singer, poet, and storyteller. Shakespeare was the most famous; they called him the Bard of Avon. He wrote poems, comedies, and tragedies. I wonder which he would have written about you." She paused for breath.

William watched her brown eyes dart around as she spoke. When she stopped, they steadied on his like a compass needle on north. "Are you from England?" he asked.

"I was born there, but we moved to Canada." She had dark hair, gathered in a bun and held in place by a tortoiseshell stickpin.

"What are you doing in Trinidad?"

"I'm on my way to my brother John. But the railroad doesn't carry through the mountains yet. I have been waiting for weeks now. They assured me in Canada that it would be through by the time I arrived. My money is disappearing like afternoon tea. My brother went to California and started a sheep ranch. But it failed and he opened a store in New Mexico last year, and asked me to come. He loves me." She winked at him. Her words were a gushing spring; her tightly laced bosom rose and fell rhythmically as she pumped them out.

"You could take a wagon over the p-p-pass, not wait for the railroad."

"I may do so yet. What I would do for protection I am sure I do not know. And how long is the road once I get over the pass? My brother is far south of Santa Fe. He writes it is pretty country. A long green valley. Sounds like Ireland to me, though of course I have never been there. Not Irish, you know."

"Yes, ma'am. It sounds peaceful, though." The food arrived: roast quail and buttered beans.

"My brother says the town of Lincoln reminds him of Canada, though as I said, I more fancy it as Ireland. How far is Lincoln, do you think? Have you been there? How much money will I need to get there? Will you take me?" She stopped, her mouth a big O. She blushed and held her palm to her lips.

William felt his face tighten in surprise. "Hoot, hoot," he said.

"Oh dear," she said. "Sometimes I just get going and goodness knows what will come out of my mouth. 'Words without thoughts never go to heaven.' Shakespeare said that. I have been watching you for days, and decided when I saw you stand down that gang of ruffians that you could be my Roland, my knight-errant."

"Your night what?"

"My knight-errant. Like in the old days of England, with fair maidens and chivalry. Do you know what chivalry is? The strong protect the weak. I think you are strong. 'O, it is excellent to have a giant's strength, but it is tyrannous to use it like a giant.'" She wound down and took a deep, steadying breath. Her eyes once more did their compass-needle dance.

"Yes, ma'am, I know what chivalry is." He added mentally, And about words without thought.

Emily ate in comparative silence after that. She picked daintily at her fowl and seemed less nervous. Her eyes did not roll around as much. William figured she had said her piece, and that maybe she had needed to steel up her nerve to do so.

"Miss Tunstall, I have been looking for a place to settle down for years. I hoped Trinidad would be that place. Now I am being paid to be here. I do n-n-not like it none, but I have not had much choice in the matter."

"'Let me embrace thee, sour adversity, for wise men say it is the wisest course.' So how does destiny deprive thee of thy liberty?" Emily's eyes twirled again.

William chewed his savory fowl, watching the dance of her eyes. He swallowed. "Dave, a man working for the Atchison, Topeka and Santa Fe railroad, made me an offer to work for him, but it is work I despise. Not taking 'no' for an answer, he tried to bribe me with room and board at this hotel, and then arranged a fight with the men of the Denver and Rio Grande to ensure that I retained no option to work for them instead. That was still not enough to get me to sign on with him; he burned down the D and RG railhead and drew me in even deeper. Now I have no recourse for no one else in town will hire me, I owe money at this hotel if I refuse the work Dave gave me, and he has left me in charge of his business here."

"Shakespeare said, 'There is nothing either good or bad, but thinking makes it so.'" She popped a buttered bean into her mouth.

William laid down his knife and fork. "Your Mr. Shakespeare is wrong. A man's honor, his given word, paying his debts—these are things that are good of themselves."

Emily's eyes stilled, fixed on William's. Her countenance drooped.

Other good things came to William's mind: helping a lady in distress, honest work, a clear conscience. "Miss Tunstall, I need to get shed of my responsibilities here first, but then I can g-g-get you across the pass at least. I can settle in Trinidad afterwards."

Her face brightened, her eyes glowed. "Oh, jolly good. Your word, then. When do you think we can leave?"

Gandy Dancers

"I will quit just as soon as I can make sure the hotel bill is settled. But the men who hired me are out of t-t-town right now. It may take a few days."

"I shall look forward to it," Emily said. She patted her lips with a napkin. "As for me, until then I shall 'give every man my ear' but few my voice."

William returned to his room and stretched out on the bed. Weary, yet he could not fall asleep. What did he owe Dave? The man paid for William's room and board, but William had never agreed to work for him for any wages. Still he had earned the money. It would be simpler to just give the money back, except William never actually saw it. And how did he give back nights of room and board? Just call it even for now? But how about from this day forward?

The next morning he went to the Topeka Lil. Five early drinkers from the Atchison were there, and as always, Sugar tended bar.

"Who do I see about closing out my b-bill at the hotel?" William asked Sugar.

"You leavin'? What about the Denver crew?"

"It is not my fight. If Dave can l-l-leave it for other business, so can I."

Sugar put down the glass he was polishing. "Dave left because you were here to handle things."

William put his foot on the rail and rested his left elbow on the bar. "Without my agreement."

Sugar grabbed a bottle from under the bar. It was rum and still sealed. "But you are here now," he said in soothing tones. "Have a drink while I tell you what's going on over at the Rio." He poured out a tumbler.

"Do not make too long a tale of it." William picked up the glass and swished the liquid around.

"The D and RG has brought in a couple of gandy dancers to start blasting out a grade."

"No concern of mine." William swallowed half his drink.

"Most likely it will ruin the toll road. That will set the AT and SF back, and probably secure the pass for the Denver."

William held his half-full glass partway to his mouth. "Woolton and McBride would have something to say about that."

"They sold the right-of-way; the toll-road business is already finished. They may lose a few months of tolls until the rails are laid, but that's not enough to get them to face down the Denver crew."

William slammed his glass to the bar top. "And I should?"

Sugar's jaw clenched, but he kept the honey in his voice. "You're on the Atchison's payroll."

"They have not actually paid me yet. If they want me

to s-step in here, then let them settle the b-bill at the hotel for starters."

"I am sure that will be taken care of when Dave gets back. But meanwhile, somebody's got to stop the Denver crew."

"By bullying them? Shooting somebody maybe? It d-d-disgusts me, Sugar." William picked up his drink and slammed it down in one swallow. He remembered something that Emily had said about a giant. And he remembered a promise to take her over the mountain. "If I didn't have need of that toll road, I would let the Denver crew blast. Hell, I would stand g-g-guard for them."

William pushed off from the bar and strode out onto the boardwalk. He looked across at the Rio. Eight men stood on the boardwalk in front of it, all nervously fingering the butts of their pistols. William thought he must have been seen entering the Lil. That meant the men at the Rio had probably started gathering the troops. Already he could be facing long odds, and who knew how many remained inside the saloon? Maybe some of them had rifles.

He called back over his shoulder. "Sugar, got any rifles?"

"Got a scattergun under the bar and a hunting rifle in the back room."

"Well, pass them out. But no shooting unless they s-s-start it."

A Civilizing Influence

William took one step off the boardwalk. The dirt crunched under his boots. An icy hammer of wind blew down from Fishers Peak. He wore a thin leather shirt over his long-sleeved flannel, and the cold air found quick entry.

He saw the men opposite him all wore long dusters or woolen jackets. That was good; the extra weight and unaccustomed binding of the confining canvas coats would slow them down and impair their aim. Only the width of the street away, William knew he could hit them from where he stood. No need to go closer and give away his advantage.

Time, though, worked against him; the cold would only get worse and more men could come.

"I hear you got plans to blast out a new route," he called to them. "I got no quarrel with that, so long as you do not touch the toll road." The words flowed smoothly from his mouth, a sure sign that the dark tornado was close.

A man wearing a dark suit and a narrow knitted tie stepped from the Rio. "You got no say in the matter." The speaker cupped his hands and blew into them.

William stared him down. "I tell you now that if the toll road is touched, you will answer for it. Not the gandy dancers, not the crew, but you, personally. You all know me—you know that I say what I mean and I do what I say."

"You can't take all of us." The man's voice was high and squeaky now.

"You will be the first and five of you will follow. After that, I will take my chances."

The nine men looked at each other, all heads swiveling one way and another with tense lips and hollow eyes. The man in the suit retreated into the Rio. The other eight unraveled like a knit tie.

"Remember what I said," William called into the Rio. "You, personally."

William returned to the Lil, angry with himself. That was as close as he had ever come to bullying someone. He didn't like it.

The scattergun was lying on the bar; the hunting rifle must have still been in the back room. He picked up the scattergun and cracked the barrel. It was unloaded. He handed it to Sugar.

"Load that. Best if someone is watching the g-g-grade. You know the crew, pick someone reliable."

Sugar's eyebrows shot up and he gaped at the scattergun. "Ya mean it wasn't loaded? Sorry, careless of me, but I'm certain it was loaded the night of the fire."

"Did somebody carry it that night?"

"One of Dave's men, I think."

William shrugged it off. "Well, load her up. I want to

hear first thing if any of the Denver men start up the p-p-pass."

Sugar nodded. "Good to have you aboard... Again... Still."

"I want to know when Dave gets back."

"You can keep a better eye on things from here than from the hotel," Sugar said, drawing a beer. "Drinks on the house while you wait."

"I will be here more often than I have been b-b-but not all the time. I do not want the boys at the Rio to get too c-c-comfortable with my movements. Let me out the b-b-back."

For the next three days, William moved back and forth from hotel to bar. He used the back doors to keep his movements unpredictable. But every evening, he had dinner with Emily. After they had eaten, he walked with Emily up and down Main Street past the wooden houses—some with picket fences—lining the boulevard.

Woolton's sheriff's office lay along this residential avenue. Peace and prosperity dwelled here, the raw energy and blood emotions of the railhead at the other end of town largely ignored.

Several of the homes showed remodeling with stone or brick courses replacing the simple earthen foundations.

Emily stopped in front of one of these. A young mountain maple graced the yard as it stood sentinel over a stone path leading to the front porch.

"A few more years and this town could look very English," she said. "I would like to live in an English-made America."

"Is that the future you hope for? A nice stone house on a genteel street in a settled land?"

"Yes. Life must be civilized and that means made orderly."

Thinking of his efforts to keep the men from the D&RG guessing, he said, "This country is far from orderly. It may be years before your dreams for America come true."

Emily smiled at him. "With men like you, William, working for the betterment of society as a civilizing influence, it won't take so long."

William shot her a hard look. Was she teasing him? "I am hardly a factor in the making of civil society."

She shook her head. "You sell yourself short. By your hand, this railroad will be completed in weeks instead of months. You cut through the impasses, get things done."

William's face reddened. "I kill people."

"And so empires are built. I do not think that in your heart you are a killer; you only do what you must. A house is not built without felling some trees."

"That is the first time I have ever been thought of as a civilizing influence."

"William, if I did not think you were, I would not keep company with you."

He smiled his appreciation at her comment, but deep in his chest, he felt hollow. He did what he had to do, but that didn't make it right.

Waiting for their food to be served at dinner on the third night, Emily said, "I wonder how John is doing without me. 'Ignorance is the curse of God; knowledge is the wing wherewith we fly to heaven.'"

She wore a black dress trimmed with red ribbons.

Like all her dresses, William thought it looked regal. "Is your brother anything like you?" he asked. "You seem out of p-p-place in Trinidad."

Emily looked around the room and then examined the front of her dress. "What do you mean?"

"You look fine, Miss Tunstall. I mean you l-l-look like you should be in a fine English manor house, not a frontier town like Trinidad."

"Of course I do not belong in Trinidad. But I was taught at Lady Ralston's Finishing School to bring the best of the empire with me wherever I go. So I am well versed in etiquette, the classics, all the important things. I even play chess. Do you play chess, William?"

"No, ma'am. Is your b-b-brother as well educated as you?"

"Better. He has a true British education. And he learned finance at our father's business in Canada. He beats me at chess." She paused, steepled her fingers. "Would you like to learn chess, William?"

"Some day. Did your brother ask you to join him to help him run his store?"

"Oh, I have no head for business. He sent for me because he misses me." She fell quiet as the food was served and slipped into a rare melancholy. "Boiled beef again?" She sighed.

"I would not expect too much in Lincoln," William said. "It is just a cow town, grown up to serve the local ranchers. Trinidad is a city of sophistication in comparison."

She stared at him over a forkful of boiled potato. "Have you been there?"

"No, ma'am, but many others just like it."

She cocked her head slightly, shot him a small frown. "William, I think you are trying to talk me out of going."

"No, Miss Tunstall. I just do not want to see you expect too much. I would hate to see you hurt."

"My brother will never fail me. Will you fail me, William?" Emily stopped eating and set her spoon firmly on the white tablecloth. "I just do not know how these railroad men can sit around all this time. Don't they have to pay those workers? I had heard that railroaders were in a great impatience, yet here they just sit. '*Tempus fugit.*' I think it was Ovid who said that. I must leave by Sunday at the very latest. By the middle of the week for certain."

William chaffed. His honesty with Emily, both about the reasons for his delay and his concern she held too high a hope for Lincoln to be the paradise she thought, had not given her the slightest pause. So if she insisted on going, he would be pleased to take her.

He had not felt so tied down since he left his home farm. After leaving home, he enjoyed the freedom to come and go as he pleased. Sure, there was loneliness, but he expected nothing else. Now obligations, even those not of his own making, trapped him. If he didn't break free soon, he'd bust.

He said, "I have been waiting for Dave, but if he is not b-b-back by next Sunday, I will see if the D and RG will pay my hotel b-b-bill just to get me out of town. I have had a b-b-belly full of this."

"That will be satisfactory. In the meantime, as one of His Majesty's rebels—Ben Franklin—once said, 'We learn from chess the greatest maxim in life—that even when everything seems to be going badly for us we should not lose heart, but always hoping for a change for the better, steadfastly continue searching for the solutions to our problems.' Come on, William. Have a go at chess. I think you shall profit by it."

16

Good News, Bad News

The next day William had a moment of hope when he found Mike Roarke, one of Dave's partners, at the Lil. Unshaven, splattered with frozen mud, the lean and mustachioed man had been riding hard; he smelled of horse and too few baths. His boots squished when he put his weight on them.

William let him finish his drink. "Dave back too?"

Mike's smile spread slowly across his chapped and tired face, as if the reddened skin grudgingly gave ground. "He's been delayed." Mike leaned back against the bar, the smile still slowly spreading. "Probably for quite a spell."

"What happened?"

"He got arrested in Kansas."

"Hoot," William said, his hand knocking a glass over. "For what?"

"Train robbery."

William took a deep breath. Still making trouble, he thought. "The Denver and Rio Grande," he said in a flat voice.

Mike shook his head. "The Santa Fe."

William's breath caught in his throat. "He tried to rob the railroad he works for?" William looked out into the street, wondering what it meant. Was he still employed? Maybe this was what he and Emily had been waiting for.

"That was Kansas, this is Colorado." Mike motioned for Sugar to refill his glass.

"So are you running things here now?" William asked, rolling his own glass in his fingers.

"I'm not stayin'. Just on my way down to New Mexico."

"I see. So the AT and SF is finished here." Relief

spread in a wave that started at William's heart and swept all the way to his fingers.

"Not hardly. We've practically got this place tied down." Mike took a long swallow.

"Then who is in charge?" William asked.

Mike stared at him. "You are."

William stared back. "That is not the way I see it. I am g-g-going to New Mexico too."

Mike clenched his jaw. "You're bein' paid by the AT and SF."

William slammed his fist onto the bar. "Then put some money on the counter. P-p-pay off the hotel. Or I am leaving."

Mike held his hands out, palms up in the age-old gesture of impoverishment. "I got nothin' to pay you with. We didn't get a cent from the train robbery."

William stepped clear of the bar. "Maybe there is a price on your head."

Mike's arm froze with his drink halfway to his lips. His eyes shot down to William's gun, and then back to his face. "Nope. No price. Not in Colorado."

William relaxed his stance. "I am not going to stay trapped in this t-t-town. You got two days to figure me a way out."

"What am I supposed to do? I'm on my way to New Mexico."

"You are going to come to the hotel with me, right now. You guarantee the b-b-bill, with your own saddle if you have to."

Mike scowled, but led the way out the door. William made him walk in front all the way down Commercial.

William and Mike entered the hotel lobby. Robert, sorting papers when they entered, stopped with one hand in the air, ledger note dangling, face hanging open in a comical stare. He swallowed hard when the two men approached the desk.

"How may I h-h-help you, s-s-sirs?" Robert's hands shook.

"How much is my bill?"

"Sorry, sir? I thought you understood that the AT and SF is paying your bill."

"Yes, what does it come to?"

"Why, nothing, sir. When you leave, we'll wire them the bill."

"You mean I can leave any time?" William laughed, slapped Mike on the back.

"Yes, sir. Will you be leaving, then? Sorry to see you go, sir." Robert's head was bobbing up and down, his words flying out in a rush.

No regret there, thought William. "I leave tomorrow morning."

Mike stepped away from the counter. "I'll be leaving before that. Maybe I'll be seein' ya, in New Mexico." His eyes were dead and empty, like dry gulches.

William had dinner again that night with Emily Tunstall. "I have things settled here. I am free to leave tomorrow," he told her over the soup.

"That's wonderful. Most men do not appreciate how well a lady can ride. I am a very good rider. I prefer Arabians, but I have not seen any here. What breed do you ride?"

"I do not have a horse. I came here by t-t-train, same as you."

"No horse? Then however are we to get over the mountain? My heavens, if I'd had a horse, I'd have ridden out long ago. This is a fine hotel, but my brother is waiting."

"What did you have in mind when you asked me to take you to your brother?"

"I thought you had horses. I mean what kind of cowboy doesn't have horses? I could go by wagon, but they are hard on the kidneys. I will be of little use to John if I get there with ruined kidneys." She blushed. "Almost let the cat out of the bag that time," she mumbled to herself.

"I always figured you would go by wagon." He picked at his plate of beans, puzzled.

"I meant to go by train. I have no idea what to do now. That's why I asked you to take me."

"I will see what I can hire tomorrow. How much can you afford?"

"My funds are running low. A fool and his money are soon parted, and I am afraid I have been four times the fool. Maybe John can wire some to me."

"I will look around tomorrow, and let you know how much you'll need."

Emily ate the main course of boiled beef in silence. Samuel brought apple pie for dessert. Dan Dement, Dave's mush-mouthed partner, entered the dining salon before William had set a fork into the pastry.

"We got trouble," Dan said, not even favoring Emily with a glance.

"I know. A train robbery in Kansas." William saw Emily's eyes flutter.

"Not that. I'm hard ridin' to catch up with Mike. But thought ya ort to know the Dirgee is hirin' a gun hand to kill ya. They're payin' five twenty-dollar gold pieces, in advance."

William wrinkled his nose. "In advance?"

"Yep." Dan grinned. "No one would face you for just a promise of money."

"Who is he?" William unconsciously looked out the window. "Is he here already?"

"Don't know. Sugar might know. I'd stick around, but I gotta catch up with Mike."

William snorted. He'd never trust Dan for help. "Yeah, you catch up with Mike. He is only a couple hours ahead of you."

William and Emily finished their desserts in silence. She kept glancing at him, her brows a question mark, but then looked away when he tried to make eye contact. He worried she could be having second thoughts. Finding out his employers were train robbers and that a gunman was in town looking for him would scare off the hardiest of women, even more so a woman of Emily's genteel stock.

She looked at him with mild reproach. "'No legacy is so rich as honesty.'" She rubbed her palm over her eyebrows. "Not that I have room to talk."

"Does it bother you that the man who pays my hotel bill is also a train-robbing outlaw?"

Emily leaned forward and cupped her chin in her hand. "A spicy stew hides bad meat. Though a man is known by the company he keeps, I believe these men have unfairly put you to their service."

A burden lifted from William's shoulders. "Thank you for your understanding."

"We can all use a little understanding at times." Emily forked a piece of apple pie into her mouth. "Are you worried about the other man? The one that rude fellow said was being paid to kill you?"

"Only until I find out who he is."

Emily's eyes softened, and a blush like early dawn on a rose touched her cheek. "If such a deed be done, best done quickly. I hope he doesn't interfere with our leaving town. William, I know you at one time hoped to make a home here in Trinidad. But I think you shall find Lincoln even better suited to settling down."

Any doubts William had about taking Emily to Lincoln vanished. And a new warm feeling sprouted from his heart.

That night he slept well, lost in pleasant dreams.

The next morning William went to the stage office. Copper was on duty. Today the clerk wore a green shade cap and his sleeves were rolled up to the elbows. He bit his lip when he saw William.

"Mister Barlow is not in yet this morning."

"I do not need to talk to Mr. Barlow. How much is a ticket to Santa Fe?"

Copper shook his head. "Mr. Barlow gave me instructions that if you came in again, he should be called immediately."

"I am just asking about the price of a ticket."

"Even so. He wants to conduct all stage business with you himself." Copper's voice slid up and down in pitch, and his eyes looked off to the side when he spoke.

"Then tell him I am here."

"He should be here in about an hour. Please come back then."

"Count on it." William left the office. As he headed to the Lil, he took the open street, walking down Commercial. Very few other people were out. Was it his imagination, or were eyes following him from the shadows? He didn't feel comfortable until he entered the Lil.

The saloon was busy. A group of six men clustered around a table, obscuring whoever was seated there. Another knot of men was at the bar, talking excitedly. They fell silent when William walked past.

William walked to the far end of the bar, put his back to the wall, and faced the open door. He waved Sugar over.

"I saw Dan last night. He said the D and RG hired a gun hand. Said you might know if he was in t-to-town yet."

Sugar's face grew pale. "How would I know that? Listen, you don't think that I—"

"I am not accusing you of anything. Dan just thought you might know."

"And you believed him?" Sugar laid both hands on the bar; they were shaking.

"Why not? You know a lot of what g-g-goes on around here. Maybe some stranger came in here, looking for me." William's tongue tingled. "Why d-d-do you look so scared, Sugar?"

"We've been friends, ain't we, William? You know I wouldna do anything against you."

Steel springs tightened in his gut. William took a half step away from the bar. "What is bothering you, Sugar?"

Sugar pointed a shaking finger at the crowded table. "Ask him."

William shifted his eyes. Chairs scraped. Men stood and parted. Through the gap, William saw Dave sitting at the table.

17

Dave Returns

D ave put his hands, palms up, out to his sides. "Don't get jumpy, partner."

William did not relax. "Where have you been, Dave?"

"Well, jail, for a little while at least," Dave said and smiled. "Me and a fellow named Ed West."

"I heard about the train robbery," William said. The other men in the saloon were standing still, silent. The air was stale.

"Not some of my better work, I will admit. Ed and I got caught by Bat Masterson right away. You know I once got chased clear across Kansas by Wyatt Earp, and he never caught me."

"Wyatt chased you?" William liked Wyatt; the man had been a friend at a tough point, and showed compassion when none had been expected. To think that Wyatt had once chased, and failed to catch, Dave salted the roots of any possible friendship between them.

"Yep. And if I had to get caught by somebody, I'm glad it was Bat." Dave leaned back in his chair.

Men murmured, shoulders dropped, and arms were held less stiffly.

"Why is that?"

Dave laughed. "Because I can talk my way out with Bat. Like I did. Told him what he wanted to know in exchange for letting me go."

"You mean you turned on your partners." William thought that he too would rather deal with Bat than Wyatt. Unlike with Wyatt, William would be willing to shoot Bat, and that kept things a little more square in any dealings with the flamboyant lawman.

Dave stopped smiling. "I gave evidence, sure. Ed

would have done the same thing, but I was quicker. Now I'm out, and he's in jail."

"What about Dan and Mike?"

"They didn't get caught, and they owe me for that. Best if they stay out of Kansas for a while." Dave picked up his glass and drew a long draught. The men in the saloon began talking to one another again; the mood, which had been as tense as air before a prairie storm, relaxed.

"So you are back here? The Atchison just looks the other way when you try to r-r-rob them?" William felt the steel springs unwind a little, though his thoughts remained confused.

"Sure. They like the work I'm doing here." Several men laughed. A wave of cold air blew in as someone came through the door.

"Your work here . . ." William made no attempt to hide his contempt. "Since you are back to do your work, I will be leaving."

Dave rose to his feet. "You might want to hold off just a bit. The gunfighter you were asking Sugar about? He's here already."

William saw Dave's hand near his gun. "You?"

Dave's mouth fell open. He shook his head. "Why would I want to kill my best man?"

William heard Sugar let out a held breath. That explained why the bartender had been so nervous. He had also thought Dave was the hired gun.

William's shoulders relaxed. "Then who?"

Dave shrugged. "I just know he's already in town."

"If the Denver wants to get r-r-rid of me, why send someone to kill me? I make it no secret I am leaving," William said, rubbing his neck with his left hand.

"Maybe they think you'll show up again, later," Dave said, pulling the makings of a cigarette from his vest pocket. "The battle here's near over, but there's still the Royal Gorge. Bat told me about it; both sides are recruiting."

"I have no intention of staying in Colorado. I am heading for New Mexico."

Dave rolled his cigarette. "Too bad—I's hoping you'd come along."

William shook his head. "Since you are back, and things are about d-d-done here, I will be leaving." He leaned over to shake Sugar's hand. "No problems between us. Thanks for everything."

"Watch out for strangers. There's still the matter of those gold pieces," Sugar said.

"I will keep to the hotel. Send word if you can."

William started down the deserted Commercial Street. The cold was like a sepulcher, the shadows starker. Thin sunlight reflected off the glass in the upper-story windows. They looked like eyes staring down on him. The street was an unturned grave. Somewhere a man stalked him—maybe with a rifle— and even now had William framed in his sights. William's heart pounded. Every step echoed hollowly in his jaw. He fought a constant urge to turn around and look behind him.

Five strides to the hotel, the prickling of his palms joined to each ponderous footfall. Sound retreated as blood rushed through his ears. The hotel porch became the whole world. He stopped in front of it, convinced that would be his last step. He forced himself on.

18

The Pass Is Closed

Light-headed, William didn't breathe until the hotel door closed behind him. He stood just inside the door, letting his pulse slow and his breathing return to normal. His light-headedness cleared. He sank into his favorite chair and his body shook. Many times he had faced down the guns of another and never had this reaction. The tornado whirled inside him with no place to go, threatened to rip him apart. He resolved to never again put himself in such a position.

Robert the clerk looked at him briefly, shrugged, and went back to scratching in the ledger.

Waiting until the street filled with people, William returned to the stage office after noon, hoping the crowd made an ambush less likely. Mr. Barlow waited on him. Tom stood nearby, arms crossed across his chest, but looking twitchy as a cow's tail.

"Still can't help you out with a job," Mr. Barlow said.

William raised a hand to stop him. "I did not come for that. I want two tickets to New Mexico."

"Where in New Mexico?"

"Lincoln."

Mr. Barlow reached beneath the counter and withdrew a large book. He flipped open the brown clothbound cover and leafed through it. Ruled like a ledger, William could not read the upside-down entries.

"Let's see, don't get many requests for that." Barlow's finger stopped running down the lines, targeted an entry. "You need to change in Santa Fe, and take the stage for Alamogordo. It'll run through Lincoln."

William thought that sounded far away. "How much for two?"

"Thirty-five to Santa Fe, and twenty additional to Lincoln, each. That includes twenty-five pounds of baggage per passenger."

William did the sums. "When do you need the money?"

Mr. Barlow closed the book. "The pass is closed now. Maybe next week if we don't get a big snow."

"The wagons are crossing now."

"Some are, it's true. But that's freight, and this is people. The Company cannot guarantee the safety of the passengers unless the pass is open."

"I will let you know. In the meantime, send word to the hotel if things change."

William left to return to the Sherman. This time there were only a few people between the stage office and the hotel. His skin crawled as he moved down the street. He stayed on the boardwalk, as close to the side of the buildings as he could. He felt like a coward. He knew he could never take another week of this. Though

Emily had told him she would not go by wagon, he would have to convince her.

He waited for Emily in the parlor. If unable to convince her to go by wagon and not wait for the stage, he wondered if Emily would object to two full fares. One hundred ten dollars was a lot of money. Ten more than the price someone had put on his life. He shivered and remembered the old wives' tale, which warned someone had walked over his grave.

He felt a spasm coming; he rubbed his hands together, but his shoulder twitched anyway. He was not afraid of a gunfighter who would stand up in front of him. However, as his reputation grew, a killer would try to ambush him. And this payment in advance invited murder since the killer would not have to identify himself afterward to collect the money. William feared he would never survive the week. The only solution was to smoke out the hired gun, settle it first.

Emily came down the stairs. She was wearing a yellow dress with black trim, and a black shawl wrapped around her throat. He liked yellow; it was a good change from black. How many dresses did she have? Would she have trouble staying within the twenty-five-pound limit?

Her eyes flashed a deep reflection of the lamplight. William waited for Samuel to seat her at the table, and then seated himself. A silver locket, hanging at her throat, picked up the lights in her eyes. She smelled of rose water.

He leaned forward. "Miss Tunstall, the stage will not run for at least a week, maybe longer, until the pass is clear of snow." He ladled soup from the tureen and passed it to her.

Her right hand, white and delicate, fluttered at her bosom. "Oh dear. I do not like this town. I feel trapped here. I am afraid something horrible will happen if I stay. Our fate is not in our stars, but in ourselves. And there is that man looking for you, looking to kill you."

William reached for her left hand, held it in both of his. "I will be all right. We will find a way out." Her hand lay soft and warm in his. The muscles on his chest tightened.

Emily's brows drew together. She looked at their clasped hands. She smiled, let her hand linger for two heartbeats, and then withdrew it.

William let out a slow breath. He said, "We could try riding over in one of the freight wagons. I could buy a wagon and dr-dr-drive us across myself." He tried his soup; it was too spicy. He wanted something sweeter.

Emily looked up, mouth open in her round face, a circle within a circle. "All the way to Lincoln?"

"Over the pass. We should not have any trouble g-g-getting a stage once we are in New Mexico."

"What is the fare?" She set aside her soup, fiddled with her napkin.

"Thirty-five per passenger to Santa Fe. Another t-t-twenty to go on to Lincoln, including twenty-five pounds of b-b-baggage. That is, if we wait and go by stage. I did not ask about a wagon, but it should be cheaper." William expected Emily to pause to add up the fares, and know by her answer whether she still intended to have his company.

"So a hundred and ten," she said nearly as fast as

William could pull his gun. "A simple solution if we had the time. But I cannot wait a week."

"Do you have that much? Remember, a wagon might be cheaper."

"No, I am certain my hotel bill will consume what little I have left. I shall wire John for it. Too bad we cannot travel through the wires as well. I read a book where people could fly. Do you think we could hire a balloon?"

William laughed gently. A whimsical idea, but he knew that she meant it in all seriousness. "I never thought of that."

After Emily went up to her room following supper, William returned to the lobby. He moved a floor lamp, its brass shade heavy with *bas-relief* horses and trailing strands of black silk soft as a woman's hands. He positioned it to cast the back of the room in shadow, its flickering kerosene flame confusing the sight of anyone who entered.

William moved his favorite chair into the darker shadows, comfortably close to the rear. He had never deliberately sought out a challenger before. Now his back was to the wall. Perhaps he had overplayed his hand, made people too aware of his speed. He'd left only one way open for the killer—ambush. He hoped the gunman would come for him tonight. If not, then William would have to hunt tomorrow. Hunt for a man he did not know in a town filled with strangers.

He could keep his few friends around him, and stay out of the street. But then Sugar, Samuel, and Miss Tunstall would be in the line of fire. He could not tolerate that. And he would not live in fear, skulking about the hotel. He stared at the diamond patterns on the wallpaper, green and gold with little black centers that merged into a chaotic grey smudge beyond the lamplight.

Samuel brought him a glass of bourbon; he waved it away.

Would there be a rattle before the strike? Would the man's hands shake and cause him to miss his first shot? A thin edge to live on.

William stayed in the chair; he knew there would be no sleep tonight.

Woolton

Around three a.m. a portly man entered the lobby, testing each step with care, feeling ahead with the toe of his boot. William had seen him somewhere before. Was this the man? He inched his hand toward his revolver.

The man scanned the room, squinting in the uncertain light. He stepped farther into the parlor. The light illuminated a star on his chest. When he saw William, he flinched.

William remembered the sheriff from the first day in town; he had seemed hesitant even then about breaking up a fistfight. And absent throughout all the subsequent gunfights. A man well out of his depth. Still, this was a strange hour to be creeping into the hotel. William stood slowly, warily, deliberately putting no menace in his movements. He forced a smile. "Some trouble in the hotel, sheriff?"

The old man exhaled slowly, and William saw the tension go out of his rounded shoulders. "Did I wake you?"

"No. I thought I might be having a visitor, but I never expected it to b-b-be you."

The sheriff nodded and pointed to a chair. "May I sit? I'd like to speak with you."

William gestured at the chair, and sat down again. He took the weight on his left hip, his right overlapping the cushion. His right hand rested on the plush arm of the chair; his holster—and the revolver inside— hung within easy reach.

"Name's Dick Woolton." The man extended his hand.

William nodded, kept his hands on the arms of his chair. "The man who built the toll road?"

"And sold it. With the railroad I thought it a good time to find something else to do." Dick touched one hand to the star on his chest.

"But why a sheriff?"

Woolton yawned, stretched his shoulders. "Just sort of natural, I guess. Folks looked to me as a town leader before the railroad came. I'll give sheriffing a couple of years."

William's face twitched. He saw the sheriff smile briefly. "Been a lot going on and I have not seen much of you. Where you b-b-been until now?"

"I pretty much keep to Main Street. The railhead end of Commercial I think of as out of my jurisdiction."

William glanced at the seven-foot grandfather clock near the door. "And you wanted to t-t-talk to me now?"

"I didn't expect to find you up, but since I did, now's as good a time as any. Nice and quiet, you know?"

William grunted. "Just making your regular three a.m. rounds, h-huh?"

The sheriff let William's comment pass. "Look, I'm on the Atchison's side in this. I sold 'em the right-of-way, and I think they're entitled to being first over the pass. I've been staying out of things at the Rio and Lil saloons. Now I figure the Denver railroad's beaten, and I'm hoping you'll be moving on."

The words crashed into William's mind like a brick through a window. There it was, the expected "get out of town" from the local sheriff. Good thing he had no use for this town any longer.

"I intend to go on to New Mexico, but the p-p-pass is closed."

Woolton rubbed his upper lip with his hand, breathed hard. "Why are you here, William?"

"I have been drifting around for the last three years, t-t-taking what work I could get. B-b-but never with my gun. I hoped I could get work with the railroad here, but they hired me for the wrong reason."

"The pass won't open for another week or so, even if we don't get another big snow. Now there's another gunfighter in town, looking for you. What you professionals do is your business, but I gotta think of the townspeople."

"I . . . am . . . not . . . a . . . gunfighter," William said.

"Maybe not before, but you are now," Woolton said. He pointed at William's chest. "What was that you said—'Every fight with me is a gunfight'?"

Corralled. William sighed, feeling weary. "I was just giving fair warning, but all right. So let us 'professionals' get it d-d-done, and we will both be out of your hair. Who is this other one?"

"He hasn't exactly introduced himself to me," Woolton said. "Before the railroad I always had a pretty good idea which stranger meant trouble, and which didn't. Now, with all the rough men in and out of town . . ." He shrugged.

"Then, in the interest of your 'p-p-people,' find him and send him my way. Then we can all sit out the week in peace."

"If I were you, I'd find a good place to root, have friends at my back. Try the Lil."

"You think I have friends there?"

"Well, at least none of them are looking to shoot you." Woolton stood up. "This business belongs on Commercial Street. Wait it out at the Lil."

"I live here, in the hotel. Are you throwing me out of my room, sheriff?"

"I could, you know, for the public safety. Do you really want bullets flying around the lobby?"

Emily. And Samuel. "No. But I sleep here, so you had better help me find this g-g-gun hand tomorrow."

Woolton nodded, but William was not sure if it was agreement or farewell.

20

Visit to the Rio

William, still in the chair from which he had spoken to Woolton, saw Emily come down early for breakfast.

She wore a dress with a bright red rose print. When she saw William, she veered from her path to the dining room. "Will you walk me to the telegraph office this morning?" she asked.

"Might be safer if I did not, Miss Tunstall."

"Do not be silly. I am not asking you for protection. I just want your company."

"Hoot, hoot." Blood pounded in William's ears, and pleasant warmth spread through his gut. "I have something to take care of first."

"All right, William. I will meet you here in the parlor at ten o'clock?"

William looked at the clock. Would three hours be enough time to find and kill a man? It needed to be done, to protect Emily. But what would she think of him when it was over? "If you still want my company at ten, okay."

Her eyebrows were two little tents over her brown eyes, and then she shrugged. "Oh, for goodness' sake. 'Blow, blow, thou winter wind.' William, my admiration is not as fickle as that. Thou will find me no uncertain April day. At ten, then." She swished into the dining room.

He watched her go. The smart move for him would be to stay in the hotel, make the killer come to him. But that would put his friends in danger. And it let the killer set the timetable. Ten o'clock was not that far away. Outside, the sun was beginning the day.

William decided to go to the Rio saloon. This was a time for the unexpected. One thing to do first. "Samuel, get me a cup of coffee, please."

There was little activity on Commercial Street that morning. The air crisp as a fall apple, the sun beat hot already and the day promised warmth, and a melt. He heard the clang of hammers on steel in the distance. A crew was at work at the foot of the pass. William smelled the faint tang of creosote over the earthy aroma of cow manure.

He walked up the boardwalk on the Rio side of the dirt street. He did not wear spurs, and the creak of the boards was the only sound that marked his passage. Facing down whatever threatened him, he felt his old self: alert, alive, with none of the previous day's hollow-chested feeling.

He approached the Rio. Voices, the clink of glass, and thump of wood came from inside. He laid his hand on the batwing saloon door.

William pushed inside.

The bartender was the first to see him and dropped the glass he was polishing. Someone laughed. Then a hush swept through the room, like wind through prairie grass.

William watched the bartender's eyes. He saw them cut in a quick glance to a hatless man sitting at a table in the center of the room.

Nearly everyone he saw wore a gun, but no one reached for theirs. Sweaty faces and staring eyes followed his movement. William walked to the table, the green felt top of which looked like cropped grass. The hatless man gawked up at him; he was of the same size and build as William, and he was young, with sandy brown hair and a stubble of a mustache. He wore a black leather vest with a knife-shaped bulge in the pocket. But no gun.

William squinted down at him.

The man rubbed his chin, and smiled. "Well, so the mountain comes to Mohammed," he said.

"What do you mean?" William asked.

"I was just asking these men how I could meet you. And here you are." The young man's eyes sparkled and matched his broad grin.

William's eyes narrowed. "You c-c-could have found me faster by asking over at the Lil."

The young man slapped a hand on the table. "That's just what they said. Advised me not to go, though. They tell me you're a holy terror."

William's shoulder spasmed in an awkward shrug, and his lip curled. He snorted. He drew a quick breath to steady himself, and the indrawn breath made a *snork* sound.

The onlookers gasped. The young man laughed. "I guess it's true, then."

"Yes, it is true." William pointed with his chin at the man's gunless waist. "Why are you looking for me?"

"I'm a reporter for the *Denver Post*. My name is Kendrick Washburn." He reached into his vest.

William snapped his gun out and leveled it at the man's head.

A white-faced Washburn froze.

"Go very slowly," William said.

Washburn used two fingers to remove a pencil from his pocket. "I came down to Trinidad to talk to you for a story I am writing."

"You sure picked a day for it. Stick around and you will have a lot to write about."

William turned to address the saloon in general. "I hear someone else is looking for me. Someone with five twenty-dollar g-g-gold pieces. Is he here?" He swept the room with his eyes, but no one would hold his gaze. "Get word to him. I will be out on the street at nine a.m. Mr. Washburn, have d-d-dinner with me at the hotel this evening."

William's eye swept the room one last time; then he turned his back on the reporter and headed for the door. He kept his gun in his fist until he was on the street again.

He crossed the hard-packed dirt to the Lil. He saw faces lining the window, staring at the Rio, and him. The men standing at the saloon door stepped back with the swing of the batwing doors as if they were attached to the wood. He looked at the clock on the wall. Almost eight o'clock. "I'll have a hot rum, Sugar. I've g-g-got an hour to kill, but I want just the one."

Waiting for the Showdown

William took his drink to his usual position at the end of the bar, facing the door with his back to the far wall. The saloon began to fill with men. Sugar tapped another barrel, the striking of his wooden bong starter ringing like spikes in a railroad tie. Fresh hops scented the room.

Commotion in the street drew his attention. The northbound stage, pulled by four horses, clattered past.

A man in cotton work clothes and a soiled neckerchief banged his half-finished beer down on the bar. "I guess the stage will be out of business soon." He seemed pleased.

"Because of the railroad?" asked his drinking partner, a man with long bushy sideburns.

"Sure. Pull a lot more freight, and take more passengers faster and safer than the stage."

The second man shook his head, setting his whiskers to dancing. "The railroad don't go everywhere."

"I say if the railroad don't go there, it ain't worth going to."

The man with the sideburns lifted his glass. "For us, anyways."

The clock hands made their slow circle. William hooted occasionally. Though he did not know who he was about to face, he was not afraid. There was only one thing he completely trusted about his body, and this was it.

He imagined the challenge running from mouth to mouth throughout the town. No doubt by now the killer had heard it. Perhaps someone had told him directly, knowing who he was. People would begin to gather along the street to see the fight. That would force the gunfighter into the open, for he couldn't hope to escape a murder charge if he fought from ambush in front of so many witnesses.

He thought more about what came afterward—Miss Emily. Now *there* was uncertainty. He felt more vulnerability with her than from a dozen gunmen. A frown from her would smash his heart more surely than a bullet.

What if she heard of the challenge? Might she watch? He had never killed anyone in front of Emily before. What would she think of him after she actually witnessed a showdown? Was it right for him to care? Her touch brought a warm excitement, but was it fair for him to want her close when being so put her in danger?

After the showdown, it could be different. The stalking killer gone, he could enjoy her presence. Trinidad held nothing for him it was clear. But Lincoln? She had invited him to settle there. She already had family in that town; maybe he could find a place of peace with them.

And maybe a place with Emily? Too soon to set his sights on much more there.

What did she think of him, feel for him? She continued to spend time with him. True, she needed his help, but it was a beginning. He had no practice at reading women. He'd grown up with Eve, his younger sister. He had never been able to fully understand her thoughts and moods. He wondered if she were still on the farm in eastern Kansas, or if she had a husband yet. Poor Eve, if still with his father.

How could he hope to understand Emily? What did he know of her? Sure, she had not run off at first sight of him, but then she was trapped here, same as he. Would that change when she saw him kill someone? He couldn't let that thought linger; he could not afford doubt to slow him down now. He would face that question when the time came.

When the clock hands showed a perfect right angle, he moved away from the bar and toward the door. The many conversations around him cut off between words in a knife edge of silence. He smelled freshly spilled beer on the bar.

He stood in the doorway to study the street. A crowd billowed outside as William saw people move forward and then shrink back, dancing, he supposed, on the twin feet of excitation and fear. The center of the street remained empty: an oblong field of honor to parade the heroic and the foolish.

William stepped off the boardwalk and into the arena.

The crowd ticked, its mainspring wound past tight. Cries of "Where is he?" and boos and catcalls swelled.

The moment was near. His opponent would surely step from the crowd at any second. Honor, the western code, call it what one will, made it inevitable. The crowd faded from his consciousness; he saw only the street, the empty street. He waited.

The Telegraph

Shouts and boos from the crowd once again penetrated his consciousness. The crowd was dispersing, evaporating from the back edges in spits and frowns. The gunfighter had refused to face him. The hired killer had no honor, and that meant trouble. A man without honor was a true outlaw. And a very dangerous man.

William stalked back to the hotel. He heard the fading noise of the dispersing crowd and machine noises from the railroad camp—sounds of iron and wood in conflict—but he listened for any unusual sound. He half hoped that the man would spring from ambush, and give William a crack at him. William paused before entering the hotel, looked back down Commercial Street. Still nothing. Damn.

He entered the hotel lobby. A white-faced Emily waited for him.

"Let us get a wagon, William. Just for over the pass, and then we can get a stage on the other side. It is horrible just waiting here. 'There are times when fear is good. It must keep its watchful place at the heart's controls.' Some Greek said that. John will send me the money. I do not want to stay further."

Tension left him, replaced by a light heart. Emily worried about him. She cared. No obstacle seemed too large to overcome. "I will get us a wagon, Miss Tunstall. Might take a while, though. Seems like most folks are too scared to d-d-do business with me."

"Walk me down to the telegraph office, William." She slipped her hand into the crook of his arm. "Maybe they will do business with me."

"Hoot, hoot, hoot." William's heart pounded, and he

grew warm and light-headed—not the foggy distance of a gunfight, but worse, for there was no expectation of sudden action and a release of tension. He wanted to walk with Emily, his arm in hers. But she had grabbed his gun arm, and that sent his nerves jangling. If the man he faced had no honor, then there were no bounds on his behavior. He could shoot without regard for Emily. Shoot through Emily. He disengaged her hand.

"I had best keep that arm free," he said.

She smiled, and took his left arm. "Better?" She pulled him into the street. It was a short walk up Main Street to the telegraph.

William's head turned this way and that as they walked, his eyes trying to see everywhere at once. He strove to keep his body between Emily and every shadow hiding an imagined gunman. It gave him an awkward gait and increased his stumbling.

"My goodness," Emily said once they entered the telegraph office. "Are you feeling all right, William?"

"Guess I am not used to walking with a lady on my arm, ma'am."

Emily smiled and shook her head, then turned to talk with the operator.

William loitered by the door, taking in every nuance of his surroundings. The wood stove gave off a circle of heat that did not reach the entrance. The counter smelled of fresh pine; the inside of the office had not been painted. A woolen horse blanket hung in the window as a curtain. Through the clerk's teller-like window he saw the telegraph machine, stark black and dangling coils of wire. It clacked, but the operator kept his back to it. The sound was foreign—no rhythm but not random either. Amazing that Emily could turn those taps into money.

You could send a wire for anything, he thought. Anything. Somebody had to send for the gunman, probably used this very telegraph. William stared at the operator and thought of hidden faces. He'll talk. People are afraid of me. But not yet, he thought, wait until Emily is finished. He broke out of his reverie at a touch on his arm.

"William? Are you sure you are all right?" Emily looked at him, pinched her lip with her teeth.

"Yes, ma'am, I am fine. Did you get the wire sent?"

"I shall have to wait for an answer. They must send a runner at the other end to find John."

"Should we come back?"

Emily looked at the clock on the wall, frowned. "I think we have time to see about a wagon."

"I need to have a talk with the telegraph operator first, Miss Tunstall. Do you mind waiting?"

She crossed her arms at her waist and turned to look out the window. "Surely."

William leaned over the counter to quietly ask the operator, "Do you keep a record of the wires you send?"

Scented balm slicked the man's sparse hair, sweeping it across his scalp in a comma. The operator's face, though, was a big O of shock. "Yessir. Money changes hands, we keep a record."

"Do you know who I am?"

The clerk swallowed hard, nodded.

"Has anyone sent a wire concerning me?"

"I can't say, sir."

"Cannot or will not?" William's chin spasmed to his right three times.

A bead of sweat formed on the clerk's upper lip. "Both. I don't remember every wire. And if I did, the content is confidential."

William looked over his shoulder at Emily. She was still looking out the window. He turned back to the clerk, smiling as if about to confide a secret. "I think you would remember, or does someone hire a k-k-killer every day? Has anyone wired about me?" William kept his voice soft and friendly. He knew his eyes carried the menace.

"Not that I know of," the clerk said. He pulled a handkerchief from a waist pocket and wiped his brow.

"Okay," William said with nonchalance. "If I find out differently, I will be b-b-back to see you." William turned to Emily. "Ready, Miss Tunstall?"

They walked toward the freight office. William kept a smile on his face, his right hand clear, but he felt ashamed. *Now* I *have become the bully*, he thought. This town was changing him.

Emily did the talking at the freight office as well. A chubby man, dirty sleeves rolled up to his elbows, attended her. This man and Emily sat at a desk choked with stacks of papers. The stacks were no longer neat, as slips strayed from one to another, or hid in between, their edges curled, their flat planes creased. As Emily talked, the man's hands were never still, sorting through one stack or another. He sometimes frowned at Emily, or glanced over at William. Several times he shook his head negatively.

Emily turned to look at William over her shoulder, frowning. William stepped forward, steadied her chair so she could stand. "Come, William," she said in clipped tones. He followed her into the street.

"So many fine young gentlemen," she said in a harsh timbre. "I begin to despair, William. Who in town sells horses? On a horse a person is mistress of her own fate. I am an excellent rider, though admittedly I have never ridden over a mountain before."

"No wagon, then?"

Emily's jaw clenched; then she said, "The freight man refused to even consider it. Said he wouldn't hear of shipping a woman like freight. I explained it was just to New Mexico; he said that made it even worse. What sort of reputation does this New Mexico have?"

"It is pretty lawless, Miss Tunstall. You should not try it alone. I do not ride well, but I will find four horses."

"Four?"

"Yes, ma'am. We ride two, pack two. We could lose one over the pass."

They were passing the telegraph office again. Emily tapped her chin with a finger. "How much will it cost?"

"About a hundred dollars per horse, including all the gear."

"Oh dear, I should have asked John for more. I shall wait here for his answer, and wire back immediately. Will you sit with me?"

"Hoot." William bit down on the inside of his cheek, clenched his left fist until the tic stopped. "It is dangerous, Miss Tunstall. Someone may start shooting without caring who else is around."

Emily sniffed. "Not in full daylight, surely."

"I hope you are right, ma'am. B-b-better not sit too close just in case."

The Reporter

William and Emily entered the telegraph office again; the clerk with the slick hair would not make eye contact with William. A wooden bench sat against one wall, leaving a clear space in front of the cage.

"Do you have a chair for the lady?" William asked the clerk.

The clerk scowled but rolled out his stool from behind the counter.

William frowned at the offered chair. "This stool does not look very comfortable, Miss Tunstall," he said.

"Have a seat on the bench; I will stay here by the door."
When she sat down, William rolled the stool into one
of the front corners, and arraigned the woolen curtain
to block the view from the street. He could see out the
window, but he could not be seen by anyone unless they
entered the office.

The clerk huffed as he went about his business. Boards
creaked under his feet. He walked to the window and
looked out, turned to stare at William for a moment.
Then he looked at Emily and spread his palms open in a
shrug of his wrists. His face slicked with sweat, the
overweight man pursed his lips, tongue clicking on the
roof of his mouth as he returned to his cage.

The minutes passed; William nearly fell asleep, saved
by the sudden clacking of the telegraph. This is not
good, he thought. Too much tension, too little sleep, his
faceless enemy stalking, wearing him down. William
tired of playing the waiting game, but how to flush out
the hired gun? He'd already refused one challenge to his
honor. But waiting here, watching the street, wasn't the
answer.

"Miss Tunstall, maybe we should go b-b-back to the hotel."

"Be no bother to send someone for you when we get an answer," the clerk said before Emily could speak. "I mean, ma'am, how long do you figure to wait? We might not hear till tomorrow."

Emily locked eyes with William. "If you think it best, William." Her voice was calm and measured.

"I believe you will be safer indoors," William said. "I need to rest."

Emily turned to the clerk. "You will be sure to have my money brought over immediately." She locked her arm in William's and accompanied him into the street. "Do not worry, William. I am certain John will send me some funds soon, and then we shall buy horses and leave this town."

"We have not found any for sale yet," William pointed out.

"You rest. I shall take care of that. I am a good judge of horses, and an excellent horse trader. I have studied all the bloodlines." They passed an alley leading to the lots behind the buildings. She squinted and craned her neck as she peered at a corral. "I wonder where they keep the good ones."

"If you say so, ma'am. It will d-d-do no harm for you to ask around. But do not agree on price."

Emily frowned at William.

"At least not until we hear from your brother," he amended.

William tried not to repeat the awkward walk of that morning, attempting to keep all distracting thoughts out of his mind as he stayed alert for movement, a suspicious shadow, the slow opening of a door.

Emily walked without speaking; she seemed lost in her own thoughts.

William and Emily entered the hotel to find Kendrick Washburn sitting in the lobby.

The reporter rose, a notebook and pencil in his hands.

Emily whispered. "That man looks a little like you, William."

With a sudden pang, William took his arm from Emily's hand and stepped toward the young man. "Later, Mr. Washburn."

"Please, call me Kendrick," the reporter said. "We're having dinner at nine tonight, I believe." He smiled in a genuine show of friendship, and a little kernel of affection for the man sprouted in William. Kendrick continued, "I'm here to talk to your lovely companion."

The kernel stopped sprouting, young wheat in a spring freeze. "Huhnn huh."

Emily put her hand on William's shoulder and stepped behind him. She addressed the reporter over William's shoulder. "Do I know you?"

Kendrick glanced at William, waited a moment. "Allow me to introduce myself. I'm Kendrick Washburn, investigative reporter with the *Denver Post*. I'd like to interview you for the paper, ma'am."

"I am Emily Tunstall. I am pleased to meet you if you are a friend of William's. I shall see you at dinner, then, surely."

Kendrick kept a smile on his face. "Please, Miss Tunstall. I wanted to get some background before then. I need to craft my time with William."

"Mr. Washburn, anything I have to say to you will be

with William present. And right now he has some other pressing business." She turned to William. "Do you not?"

William smiled, his heart skipping sideways in his chest. Emily's response reassured him that Kendrick was no threat for her affection. Now perhaps the reporter could be a friend. "We will see you at dinner, Kendrick."

"Just a few words. Who doesn't want to see their name in the paper?"

"Me, for one," William said.

Washburn shrugged, pocketing his notebook and pen. "William, I hope you have no objection to my asking around town about you before then. I need to post something today."

An idea occurred to William, a way to flush out his would-be killer. "I have a good story," William said. "There is a gunfighter looking for me. Find him and interview him. While you have the chance."

Washburn beamed. "What a great idea. Who is he?"

William shook his head. "You were there this morning. You heard me challenge him. You saw that he did not meet the challenge." William caressed the butt of his revolver. "I do not know who he is. You are the investigative r-r-reporter. Investigate."

The Tornado Comes to Dinner

After Washburn left, Emily said, "You should rest now. Try to sleep until dinner tonight. 'Sleep, perchance to dream.' Do your dreams frighten you?" She drew a deep breath, cupped her cheek in her hand.

William smiled. Her eyes were the brown of a deep-forest pool in autumn, flecked with golden leaves. "I dream like most men, I guess."

Emily gave him a brief nod of acknowledgment, then turned away. "What do you think of Mr. Washburn?"

"I hope we can be friends. I have not had many. I hope he is a good investigator. If he can find the man who has been paid to kill me, then Kendrick and I can be great friends."

Emily's palm flew to her cheek. "Oh, William. Do you think Mr. Washburn is in any danger? You sent him to look for a killer."

"Not *his* killer. The bounty hunter would not want to tip his hand by killing Washburn. Sooner or later the man will have to make his move, and if Kendrick Washburn can dr-dr-draw him out sooner, then so much the better."

"'Best-laid schemes o' mice an' men gang aft agley.'" She sighed. "See you for dinner at nine."

"Maybe I will find out the name of the killer then."

William went to his room and lay on the bed. His back hit the bedding, and it felt as though he sank right through the ticking into a deep slumber.

When he woke, it was dark outside. He jumped from the bed and rushed out his bedroom door.

From the top of the stairs he could see the grandfather

clock in the lobby. The time was 8:15. He sighed in relief and returned to his room. William lit the lantern and studied his face in the mirror.

He ran his fingers through his mussed brown hair, patted it back into place. It did not stay put. His hair needed a brush, he decided.

He tried to see himself as Emily saw him. His face remained youthful, unscarred, darkened by the barest shadow of a beard. His eyes were those of an older man, and bore testament to trouble. He asked himself if Emily thought him handsome. The corners of his mouth twitched suddenly. Probably not, he thought wryly.

William put on his other shirt, brushed his pants. Washed his face and combed his hair. Strapped on his gun. He went downstairs when he heard the clock chime nine.

He walked through the lobby and into the dining parlor. Emily, who was wearing the blue-and-white print dress, was already there. With Kendrick Washburn.

William's heart rose in his throat. What was she doing with him? She had promised not to talk to the reporter until he was present.

They were seated in front of the window, Emily facing the street and Kendrick facing Emily. Emily talked and the reporter scribbled rapidly. Emily laughed, and Kendrick looked up from his notes and laughed with her. Were they laughing at him?

They knew each other!

William walked toward them. Emily stiffened—apparently saw something in the window. Had it been his reflection? Was she embarrassed to be caught with Washburn? His tongue tingled. Was his dark tornado about to break loose? And do what, shoot Washburn?

"Eeek hoot." William stumbled, clutched a chair for support. He felt the whipping wind of the internal storm, and himself losing his grip.

A gun barked. Glass shattered, and William snapped back to the present. His unfired revolver remained in his holster. He stood, taking in a series of rapid images. Kendrick sprawling across the table, knocking it into

Emily, grasping at the edges, sliding to the floor. Emily crying out, her hands flying to her face, toppling backward.

"No!" William screamed, and he sprinted to the bodies, his own safety forgotten. Emily—shot. The tablecloth smeared red. Glass shards littered the floor. Cordite hung in the air. Emily's face bloodied.

He saw someone through the shattered glass of the window swinging a revolver in his direction.

The tornado descended.

Bad Eyes and Bad Luck

William drew and fired, even as he threw himself on top of Emily. The dark tornado lasted less than a second. He felt Emily beneath him, his mind all too alert, threatening to shatter like glass. His worst fears realized—Emily dead.

A hand pushed on his belly. Emily struggled beneath him.

"William, get off. I can't breathe."

William pushed himself away, banged into the table. "Alive?" he gasped. He took a deep breath of relief. "You are alive," he said. "Are you hurt?"

"I shall be quite fine if you let me catch my breath." Emily struggled to sit up, her face pale. Her dress was askew; its blue-and-white flower pattern had new red blossoms. Blood had sprayed across her face as well, and her chin bled. "Where's Mr. Washburn?"

William clasped her arm, helped her to her feet, and steadied her. Then he pointed to Kendrick Washburn.

Emily sagged into him when she saw.

A red crater bubbled blood from Washburn's back. The gun-shot man moaned, tried to move, his hands sliding ineffectually in the spreading pool of blood beneath him.

All around William, confusion crescendoed. People pushed and shoved, all talking at once. Someone sent for the doctor. He heard someone in the street shout, "He's been shot."

William pulled Emily away and helped her to a chair in a quieter corner. He dabbed at her chin with a napkin. Splinters from a ricochet after the bullet went through Washburn? Flying glass?

"Oh, William, I saw him," Emily said, taking the stained cloth from William. She held it gingerly to her chin. "I saw him through the window when he fired. Why did he shoot Mr. Washburn?"

"Maybe Washburn found out something. Did he say anything to you?"

Emily shook her head, some color returning to her face. "I was doing most of the talking. I was waiting for you and he just sat down. He has such a way about him, but I should never have let him get me started."

"He did have a way about him. I felt it too," William said. He didn't voice the guilt welling up. He had sent the reporter to investigate. Emily had warned him that this could have put the young man in danger, but William had not believed it. But he must have been wrong, for why else would Washburn have been shot?

William searched Emily's face for signs of reproach.

"Do you know who shot him?" Emily asked.

"I got just a glimpse. But I shot at him." William looked at the overturned table, the knot of people around Washburn, now joined by the doctor. William looked through the broken window and saw the sheriff and several men standing outside. The sheriff beckoned to him.

He turned to wipe a bit of blood from Emily's face. "Will you be okay for a minute? I want to check on things."

Emily nodded. She stared into space, smoothing the sleeve of her dress with one hand.

William walked through the lobby of the hotel. From his station behind the bar, Samuel raised a quizzical eyebrow at him. William nodded back, raised a finger to signify that he was okay and would be back to talk with him in a minute.

William stepped onto the boardwalk in front of the hotel and joined Sheriff Woolton and the group of silent men standing around a body.

The sheriff pulled at his lower lip and pointed at the body. The dead man was Copper.

Puzzled, William looked at Woolton. "Why would the clerk from the stage office shoot a reporter?"

"Bad eyes, maybe. Copper had these." Woolton opened his hand. In his palm were five twenty-dollar gold pieces.

William's throat tightened, but not in its usual tic. Was Copper a decoy? Even now he could be lined up in someone's sights. His heart pounded; the back of his neck prickled with sweat. He tried to look everywhere at once.

His shoulders shook. He backed up toward the wall of the hotel but tripped over his own feet. He went down.

William looked up at the startled faces of the men surrounding Copper's body. Someone guffawed.

Sheriff Woolton looked at him with a rictus smile that he quickly hid behind his left hand. He offered the right one to William. "Here, take it easy."

William looked at the proffered hand with suspicion, not knowing who was part of the plot and who wasn't. He strained his ears, listening for the wasp whine of a bullet.

"William?" Emily called to him from the window.

His heart stopped its runaway gallop; his jaw relaxed. William looked up into Woolton's eyes, saw only concern there. He grabbed the sheriff's hand. On his feet again, he looked at Emily framed by the jagged glass shards sticking from the sash. He nodded to her.

William plucked one of the gold coins from Woolton's hand and studied both sides of it. "I do not understand. The hired g-g-gun was Copper?"

Woolton handed him the other four coins. "Money makes people do strange things." The older man pointed through the shattered window and into the dining room to where men tended to the reporter. "I warned you about this sort of thing. An innocent man shot, probably dying. Take the money, leave town."

William stacked the coins in his hand like poker chips. He tried to hand them back to Woolton. "To help with Mr. Washburn."

The sheriff refused. "I will see to him. Just be out of town before there's any more shooting."

William shook his head. "We, Miss Tunstall and I, still do not have tr-tr-transportation. Hoot."

"You could take the train north," Woolton said.

"We are going to New Mexico." William's fist closed tightly around the coins.

Woolton stared long and hard. Then sighed. "Let me see what I can do."

William nodded, went back into the hotel where Emily waited.

The doctor continued his tending to Washburn. At his direction, four men laid the wounded reporter on an unpainted door, fresh from the mill. They lifted the makeshift stretcher and carefully carried Washburn upstairs, the sawbones close behind.

The sheriff started up the stairs after them, but turned to give a last considered look at William.

"I think this will be our final night in Tr-Tr-Trinidad, Miss Tunstall," William said.

Absent Friends

Emily smiled sadly at William. "Parting from this town will not be such sweet sorrow; I wish we did not need tarry 'til the morrow. What a tale I shall have for John. I am going upstairs now. I hope I can sleep." Her look became more desperate. "Please don't die tonight."

Hearing Emily put it into words made William feel calmer. "I am sure it is over for t-t-tonight. Maybe for good." Or will be, once he saw Barlow, William thought. "One way or another I will take you across the m-m-mountain in the morning."

William watched Emily ascend the stairs, and then looked over the parlor and the lobby. Knots of people continued talking excitedly, many casting glances his way. Through the shattered window, he saw several men carry Copper's body away, back toward the stage office. That suited William; he liked giving Barlow something to think about overnight. Soften him up a little for their talk in the morning.

Since onlookers continued to crowd the lobby, William went over to the bar to speak to Samuel.

"Are you all right, sir?" Samuel asked as William approached.

"Physically, I am fine. But my head is spinning. I am trying to make sense of what happened. I am all wound up inside."

"Care for a drink, sir?" Samuel offered, his demeanor as formal and unperturbed as ever.

William shook his head. "You do not seem b-b-bothered by any of this, Samuel."

"The hotel has a reputation to maintain. The sooner things go back to normal, the better." Samuel eyed him a moment. "Will you be leaving tomorrow, sir?"

"Hoot," William said.

Samuel smiled. "Even so, I will be sorry to see you leave, sir."

It was past midnight before William went to his room. He cleaned his revolver, took off his shirt, and rolled it up. He had a new carpet bag, courtesy of the hotel, and he placed his extra shirt carefully into it. He had the same small cloth sack of his gun supplies with which he had entered Trinidad; this he now packed into the larger case. A brush, a razor, boxes of ammo, and a few other personal items and his bag was packed, still half empty.

He set the hammer on an empty chamber and put his gun under the pillow. He lay staring at the ceiling. Was tonight's tragedy his fault? Kendrick Washburn was not shot because William had sent him to investigate. It was a simple case of mistaken identity.

But was it really that simple? Maybe just being around William was dangerous. If he hadn't invited Kendrick to dinner, the man would not have been hurt.

All William had wanted was to have a friend. Was it his lot to never experience the joy of closeness with another human being? Was it selfish for him to want what could lead others to peril?

And what of Emily? The thought of harm to her made him nauseous. Was it safe for her to even travel with him? Now that the mysterious gunman was dead, it might be safe for a while. But even that wasn't certain, for what was Barlow's role in all of this?

Sleep captured him at last. He dreamed of a stagecoach, iron-shod wheel rims spitting sparks and horses puffing in clouds of smoke. Copper sat in the driver's box; Washburn rode shotgun. In the passenger compartment, Emily clung to him and cried. Through the window he saw a hellish landscape; a yellow dog, with gold coins for eyes, ran beside the coach, keeping pace.

William woke to sun streaming through the curtains in golden light. He looked through the window toward the stage office. The deserted street looked cold and stark. He dressed and filled his revolver's one empty chamber. He slid the Colt into the holster and went downstairs.

Woolton and Emily waited separately in the lobby. She wore a blue shawl and blue-and-white bonnet. A portmanteau hunkered at her feet. William eyed it dubiously. That will never fit on a horse, he thought.

"Good morning, Miss Tunstall. You are all p-p-packed, I see," he said, going to her before acknowledging the sheriff.

Emily's face puckered in confusion for a moment, and then she waved a hand at the luggage at her feet. "Not all, but you can start with this."

"Hooty," William said. "Are we still planning to travel by horseback?"

Emily smiled for a moment and then broke into tears. "I will just leave everything for the hotel; maybe they will reduce my bill. Oh, William, I am so confused. I just can't think straight after last night. Do you know that the gunman thought Mr. Washburn was you? Because he was sitting with me? I got that man killed."

"It was not your fault, Miss Tunstall." He wanted to comfort her, could think of little to help. "I can settle your hotel bill," William said, though he knew it sounded heartless. He pulled five coins from his pocket, was afraid it just made matters worse.

"That is very kind of you, but I am certain the telegram will arrive today with my funds." Emily sniffed, wiped her eyes with a handkerchief.

"Waiting even that long could be dangerous."

The sheriff approached. "Mr. Barlow wants to see you. He asked me to bring you by the office."

"I want to see him as well."

Emily touched his arm. "You will be careful? His clerk tried to kill you last night." She stared hard at the sheriff, then looked away, ready to cry again.

William smiled. "Of course. I have the sheriff to protect me."

Woolton gave him a sidelong glance. "There will be no trouble. Barlow asked me along for his own protection, I believe."

"How is Mr. Washburn?" William asked.

The sheriff motioned for William to walk with him, and ran an age-spotted hand over the sparse hair above his ears. As they stepped from the hotel and away from

Emily, Woolton said, "He died earlier this morning. He was able to talk some at the end. He asked me to contact his family. His father's a wealthy judge in Massachusetts, and two of his brothers are lawyers."

Sadness for the loss of something rare in his life stung William's eyes. "I liked him. I think we could have b-b-been friends." He stared down at the dirt as they walked up Commercial.

"I didn't think your kind made friends," Woolton observed.

27

Quick Answers

The sheriff may not be much good with a gun, but he still shoots pretty straight, William thought. Pained, he walked in silence until arriving at the stage office.

Inside, the window to the clerk's cage was closed. Tom, Bart, and Jasper, all heeled with six-shooters, stood frowning in the outer office. Barlow stood at the door to his inner office and waved William and Woolton in.

William refused the proffered chair. The stage owner rubbed his hands together nervously and looked at the sheriff as if for support.

"First, let me say how much I regret what happened last night," Barlow said at last. "I had no idea that Copper was capable of such a thing."

"Why did he do it, Barlow?" William said. He was aware of the sheriff standing to the side with his arms folded across his chest. "Who put him up to it?"

"I don't know. It had nothing to do with my stage line, or me, I assure you," Barlow said with a catch in his voice.

William looked at him steadily, challenging the businessman to say more.

"I had nothing to gain," Barlow went on. "I have always favored the Atchison."

"Maybe you wanted the war between the railroads to continue," William said, glancing at Barlow's three guards. "A nice long standoff suits your p-p-purpose best. And you saw me as the deciding piece, best removed from the board."

Barlow drew back in alarm. "You can't think that. If I didn't want you around, I would have just sold you a ticket when you asked."

"But the pass was closed, and the m-m-matter looked to be settled before it reopened."

Sweat broke out on Barlow's brow, and he held his hands up, palm out, in a placating gesture. "It wasn't like that." He turned to Woolton. "Sheriff, please tell him it wasn't like that."

"I've got no proof you were involved," Woolton said. "And there are others who could have paid Copper to kill this man. We may never know. However, things are settled between the railroads as a result of this past week's activities. The Denver crew is pulling out; the Atchison is laying track over the pass. And no one wants to stick around for an investigation." The sheriff turned to William. "You don't want to stick around, do you?"

"What about Mr. Washburn? There should be some justice for him."

"Mr. Washburn is dead, and the man who shot him is dead. The rest is all just bad blood that has been brewing in this town for too long. I will let it go at that, provided you leave town, William."

Anger flared in William. He scowled at Woolton. "Are you saying this is my fault?"

"I did warn you that innocent people would get killed if you stayed. Who knows where the faultfinding stops if we let it get started," Woolton said. "Best if all concerned just leave it alone. Been enough killing already."

"Washburn's death leaves unfinished business," William said. "Whether you consider the matter closed or not. There is still the matter of who put Copper up to it."

"I promise to look into it. But the most important thing is to stop the killing in my town of Trinidad. I want you to leave, William."

"I am not leaving without Miss Tunstall." William stared hard at the sheriff. "As I told you before, we are going to New Mexico. And we have no way to get there."

"I think the stage company can help with that. Right, Barlow?"

The stage owner bobbed his head. "Ordinarily, we wouldn't send the first stage across this early. But I will see what I can arrange."

Woolton beamed. "There now. See how easily everything can be settled?"

28

Wheelers

illiam heard Woolton's "easy fix" with mixed emotions. The prospect of leaving Trinidad at last, and traveling south with Emily as promised, gladdened his heart. His mind, though, threw restraining reins on such happy thoughts; there remained the unfinished business of the price on his head. Who had hired Copper? Dan had said that the D&RG had hired a gunman to kill William, and he had assumed it had been a strategy by them to take out their most powerful opposition. In that case, with the war over, William leaving town, and Copper dead, that business should be over.

However, what if there had been some other motive? Revenge perhaps? The man who had hired Copper was still active, and William felt threatened until he knew for certain that the matter was settled. And it angered him that anyone would put a bounty on his life. That amounted to being bullied at a distance. And William would not tolerate that.

He thought of staying in Trinidad a little longer to get to the bottom of this plot against him, but Emily anxiously waited for him to take her to New Mexico. And staying in Trinidad, trying to flush out the man behind Copper, would continue the danger to him, and those close to him. He hated to do it, but he would need to send Emily on without him.

Barlow shouted orders at his drivers, Tom and Bart. "Hitch up a team, put a couple of swingers in, and tie two extra wheelers to the back."

Tom and Bart hurried to obey, and William took the opportunity to interrupt the stage-line president. "Mr.

Barlow, I appreciate your getting a coach ready for Miss Tunstall and me, but I have business to conclude. It may be dangerous business, and I wish the lady to get out of town as soon as possible. I want to send her on ahead."

Barlow looked cold steel at William. "It makes no difference to me when or where the lady goes, but if you want to travel south with her, then I remind you the sheriff asked me to get you out of town as a favor to him and before you draw any more trouble. I don't trust the pass to be open this early in the year. I cannot guarantee the safety of coach and riders, and I am risking two men, one valuable coach, and eight horses to do the sheriff that favor. There ain't gonna be but the one stage."

Barlow glanced at the sky. "And it leaves within the hour, so it will make the top of the pass before nightfall. The next storm is on the way."

Woolton clapped Barlow on the shoulder. "I realize this is a big risk for you. But a bigger risk if William doesn't leave today." He paused, waited for Barlow to nod in understanding. Then, "William, if you don't leave today,

I'll have to lock you up for the sake of public safety. And where will that leave Miss Tunstall? Look, if we get more snow tonight, then it may be days before I can convince Barlow here to risk one of his stages on the pass road. You need to go, and you need to go now."

Barlow frowned at William expectantly. "So what is it to be? Is the lady going with you, or not?"

William nodded. "I will get my things. I do not have much. Give my luggage allowance to the lady."

Barlow turned to Jasper. "Go help the lady with her baggage."

William returned to his room and picked up his half-empty carpetbag. There was sense in what the sheriff had said, at least regarding justice for Washburn. Taking the stage the sheriff had arranged left some things unsettled and was not a perfect answer. But then William had seldom found answers that were.

Leaving his room for the last time, he found Emily struggling with her portmanteau in the lobby. "A man from the stage line took everything else, but I had to repack this." She frowned at the trunk.

William handed his carpetbag to her, hoisted the trunk onto his shoulders, and walked beside her toward the stage-line depot.

As they passed the telegraph office, the clerk called to Emily. "Miss Tunstall, your brother has answered your telegram." He waved her inside.

Emily turned to William. "You go on ahead; I shall be but a moment."

William considered dropping the portmanteau into the street and staying with Emily. His tongue had that be-on-the-alert tingle. But whoever was after him had nothing to gain by shooting Emily, and if this was a trap, then better she was out of the way.

"Sure, Miss Tunstall. I will meet you at the stage office." It felt dangerously wrong—both hands gripping the trunk, his back bent under the burden. But the stage office was only fifty feet away.

William imagined he must look like a turtle, plodding along with the double burden of trunk and worry. How well did the portmanteau protect his back? How slow would he be if someone cut loose on him?

Even so, he was not as afraid as he had been on his walk back from the Lil several days before. Now, his progress toward the stage drew fire away from Emily, and that felt good.

William arrived at the stage office a minute later, though it seemed many more than that. With great relief, he handed the portmanteau to Jasper, who loaded the top of the stage with the luggage. It joined four carpetbags and three hat boxes, while William kept his carpetbag with him inside the carriage.

Something else William packed aboard—the certainty that the business of the gold coins was not over. Hopefully, though, it was for the time being to be left behind in Trinidad.

By now Tom and Bart had hitched six horses to the draw tree and tied the reins of two additional horses to the rear of the coach.

Barlow helped Emily aboard. "I've done everything I can to make the trip safe for you. The two horses in the middle are my best swingers, to help pull you over the steep grade, even if the snow is axle deep. And the two extra wheelers on the back can be hitched in to give an extra pull if the snow is deeper than that."

He stepped back from the coach and pointed to the driver's box. "I'm sending Tom, my best driver, and Bart, to spell him and ride shotgun." He gave William a sideways look. "I leave you in the best hands that I know."

William climbed inside and sat on the front bench, facing backward; Emily sat on the rear bench, facing him. She kept a purse with her, and showed William the money she had received from her brother.

"The stagecoach line refused to take my money," she said. "The owner said you had taken care of it." She smiled at him. "You handled that most brilliantly, William."

William felt a tic begin in the muscles of his face, and he pinched the bridge of his nose with his thumb and forefinger. He looked nervously at Emily. A week cooped up in the stagecoach together. Would she open up to him, or ride in uncomfortable silence?

With the crack of a whip, the coach lurched forward. The compartment was painted brown, the seats covered with leather dyed green. Yellow trim outlined the window on the swing-away doors. The canvas window coverings were rolled down and sealed, and their bodies heated the compartment to cozy warmth. Emily's rosewater perfume soon dominated as they left the creosote and manure smell of Trinidad behind.

"We are off, Miss Tunstall." William hoped the tremor in his voice would be mistaken for one of his tics.

Emily cupped William's hand in hers. "It's a long trip. Call me Emily."

THE END

COMING SOON

THE NEXT BOOK IN THE CLOWN WILLIAM SERIES

Clown William and the Lincoln County War

William and Emily arrive at her brother's store, and are swept up in the infamous Lincoln County War. The one that made Billy the Kid a household name. And death a frequent guest.

About the Author

Robin Elno is a retired army colonel, semiretired psychiatrist, and full-time author. He lives in San Antonio, Texas, and is an active member of the San Antonio Writers' Guild.

uncommon publishing

We delight in publishing the non-traditional, unconventional and alternative including:

Fiction
Metaphysical
Professional and Nonfiction
Romance
Young Adult
IE Snaps

Review our list of themes and topics and perhaps they will inspire you to consider writing for original genres and audiences.

www.ingramelliott.com

www.ingramcontent.com/pod-product-compliance
Lightning Source LLC
Chambersburg PA
CBHW021012120726
47905CB00009B/2967